For Crime's Sake: When True Crime Kills

CARLA HOWATT

Published by By the Book Publishing, 2023.

This is a work of fiction. Similarities to real people, places, or events are entirely coincidental.

FOR CRIME'S SAKE: WHEN TRUE CRIME KILLS

First edition. February 17, 2023.

Copyright © 2023 CARLA HOWATT.

ISBN: 978-1778290619

Written by CARLA HOWATT.

To all the true crime YouTubers and the lawnerds (you know who you are!). You inspire me with your passion for informing, educating, and entertaining.

All names in this novel were assigned randomly and are not a reflection of anyone living or dead.

Chapter One

Standing over what remained of the two dead bodies, Detective Arthur Briggs managed to look both disgusted and resigned at the same time.

"I knew it was too quiet, but I should've known better than to say it out loud," Briggs said with a shake of his head. "When'll I ever learn?"

The Medical Examiner, Michael Cranston, arrived just as Briggs finished making his comment and began to chuckle. At an even six feet in height and an easy 220 pounds, Cranston seemed to take up half the space in the small living room.

"You said the 'Q' word out loud? Well, I guess we know who to blame this on," he teased the detective. "What do we have here?"

"It was some kind of suicide pact, and an awfully messy one," Briggs stated, looking down at the bodies of a man and woman.

"Who are they?"

"From what we can figure, if it's the owner of the house, the female is Natalie Baker, a 37-year- old YouTube content creator?" Briggs answered.

"Why the question?"

"Just wondering what the hell a YouTube content creator is?"

"Someone who creates content for YouTube."

"Gee, that helps out a whole bunch Cranston. I bet Jeff has a hard time not laughing non-stop with a husband like you," Briggs rolled his eyes.

"I have my moments," Cranston smiled distractedly as he knelt near the woman's body. "What about the male?"

"That we're not sure about. We know his name is Peter, but we don't have a last name yet."

Cranston continued to look at the scene without touching anything. He had been on the job long enough to know not to disturb things until he was given the go-ahead. In front of him lay the corpse of a woman who lay parallel to the man on her right. Both had what appeared to be a single gunshot wound to their head. Blood and brain matter was splattered to the left of the couple. A myriad of thoughts raced through his head at once. There was something here that just seemed off to him, but he needed to take a minute to figure out what it was.

"Anything?" Briggs asked, standing beside him expectantly.

"No, I need to wait a bit longer before they start reaching out to me telepathically," Cranston retorted. It annoyed him how some people seemed to think that his job was all about instinct and hunches. Sure, he relied on experience to know where to dig deeper and what leads to follow, but ultimately it was all based on science and numbers. And right now, the numbers weren't really adding up.

Briggs backed away a few feet. He knew Cranston was beginning to immerse himself in the case when he acted like he wanted everyone to leave him alone. Cranston was well respected in the community as an expert ME who had the ability to catch small things that were often overlooked by others who had far less experience. At 47 years of age, Cranston had been examining crime scenes and bodies for more than 20 years. He had seen a lot that informed the work he did. Of course, there were also things he had seen that kept him up at night, but he considered it part of the price he paid to help the families of the deceased get some answers.

After a good look at the scene, he joined Briggs who was directing a group of police officers in a search of the backyard.

"Well, the scene is a bit odd for a suicide pact," he started. Briggs knew enough to keep quiet and let him talk. "Most suicide pacts involve elderly people, not young couples. Although her being a Youtuber might support it being what we call a cyber or online suicide pact as we're finding the incidence of younger people with suicide ideations finding others of the same ilk online and agreeing to take their lives together is increasing quite a bit. But even then, they don't usually take their lives together." Cocking his head slightly, he appeared deep in thought. Finally, he broke the silence with a question: "What makes *you* think it was a suicide pact?"

"The note," Briggs answered.

"Holding out on me, are you?" Cranston asked.

"Nope, just wanted to know what you got from the scene," Briggs couldn't help but smile slightly in Cranston's direction.

"Does the note look legit?" This type of thing was more Briggs's forte than his. Cranston read bodies and scenes, not notes.

"Appears to be. It was handwritten, signed by both of them, and addressed to their families individually," Briggs said. "No sketchy printed notes or vague letters." He handed Cranston the note, which was encased in a plastic evidence bag.

Dear Mom and Becky,

Please forgive us for hurting you so badly. Understand that the pain of this world is just too much for us to bear. We have tried and tried to live in a world where there is so much evil and hate but it is too much. We thought that finding each other would make the pain go away, but instead, our love made the darkness of the world and the hatred stand out in stark contrast.

Mom, thank you for everything you have ever done for me. Please know this is my decision and there is nothing you could have done that would have changed anything. I know you love me, and I love you too. Your love was always enough.

Rebecca, the world I have been diving into has been darker and more depraved than I ever imagined possible. I just can't continue to live in a world where people act as monsters toward each other, and to children and the vulnerable. It's just too much. I love you with all my heart and please know that this is my decision and has nothing to do with anything you have or have not done.

Please forgive me.

Love, Natalie & Peter.

The letter had been written in neat cursive and signed with both Natalie's and Peter's signatures. Cranston handed the letter back to Briggs.

"How long will it be before you're ready to let me look at the bodies?" Cranston asked.

"Shouldn't be long now, we're almost done in here, although we'll continue to search the yard for a bit and then talk to the neighbors. Don't really think it's necessary, but it's policy. I'll have to make arrangements to tell the next of kin, but that doesn't affect anything here."

Cranston nodded in understanding and Briggs left the small house and headed outside. Looking down at the bodies once more, Cranston suddenly felt very old. How many bodies had he handled in his career? He really wasn't sure he wanted to know. So much waste, so much tragedy. For a moment, he caught a glimpse of the despair the two people lying dead before him must have felt.

Chapter Two

Rebecca wasn't sure why she was feeling so antsy today, but for some reason, she couldn't seem to sit still. Just as she tried to settle down to finish some of the paperwork for the house, she would pop up and wander around. It never ceased to amaze her how much time she spent on paperwork each month. Between her job as a substitute teacher and being the one in her marriage who managed the household finances, she seemed to always be sitting at her desk working on something.

But not now. Right now, she was standing at her kitchen sink, gazing out into her backyard at the bluebirds hopping around the birdbath. Her husband Jason had insisted on installing one when they first moved. He said it reminded him of his parent's home and that he enjoyed watching the birds come and go. But to be honest Rebecca couldn't recall a single time when he indulged in such a leisurely pastime. Come to think of it, she couldn't really recall the last time that he was even home except to eat, sleep or change his clothes. He was an accountant for a big company in the city and the pressure on him was intense. He had several big companies as clients and when he wasn't dealing with their accounts, he was wining and dining them.

Rebecca sighed and used her hands to pull her thick brown hair back into a ponytail. Some people insisted it was auburn, but she didn't see it; to her, it was just plain brown. She knew she was okay looking but had never felt beautiful, or even pretty. Her nose was just a tad too broad, and her freckles spread out across her face in a way that was just this side of being fashionable—in some areas, the freckles were so thick they almost appeared to join into one massive island of discoloration.

The doorbell broke her reverie and made her jump slightly. She pushed away from the kitchen sink and went to the front door. Throwing it wide, she was surprised to see two police officers standing on her step. Their somber expressions caused butterflies in her stomach to take flight.

"What is it?" she asked sharply.

"Are you Rebecca Robertson?"

"Yes, I am"

"Can we please come in, ma'am?"

Rebecca backed up to make room for the officers to enter.

"Is anyone else home with you?" the female officer with the severe blonde bun asked. Rebecca noticed her name tag said Mitchell.

"No, my husband is at work," Rebecca responded, her heart beating faster and the adrenaline coursing through her veins. "What's happened? Is he okay?"

"Your husband is fine Ms. Robertson, it's your sister we've come to talk to you about," the short, slightly heavy officer with thinning hair and a hint of pimples along his jawline responded this time. "Is your sister Natalie Baker?"

"Yes. Yes, it is. Has something happened to her? Is she okay? Oh God!"

"We're sorry to have to tell you but early this morning your sister was found dead in her home," Officer Mitchell said in a gentle voice.

Rebecca dropped onto the couch, her legs giving way, no longer able to hold herself upright. She felt as though a dome had been lowered over her, muffling all the voices and noises around her. She knew the officers were talking to her, but she couldn't hear what they were saying. Not that she was focusing on them. Her mind was numb and all she could think was that Natalie was dead. Natalie. Vibrant, energetic Natalie. Her baby sister who loved life and wasn't afraid to take risks to live a life that was meaningful to her. Her beautiful sister, Natalie.

She looked down and there was a glass of water in her hand. Officer Mitchell was sitting beside her with a box of tissues. She was looking at Rebecca as though she was waiting for an answer to a question.

"What?" Rebecca asked, confused.

"Is there someone we can call for you?" the officer repeated.

"Call? No. There's just Natalie. And my husband, but he's busy at work," she explained.

"I'm sure he would want to come and be with you, to be here for you."

"I don't want to bother him," Rebecca insisted. She knew he would come if she asked, but she hated to add any more stress to his life. He put in so many hours and she didn't want to set him back in his work anymore than necessary. She could handle things herself.

"If you're sure," Officer Mitchell said, hesitantly. "I have a phone number for you to call, it's the number on the back of my business card. It's for the Sheriff in Spenser, he'll be able to answer any questions that are sure to come up."

Rebecca watched the officer attempt to hand her a business card, but her arms didn't seem to be working properly. Finally, the officer set the card down on the coffee table.

There was a loud crackling sound from the direction of the door and Rebecca jolted and swung her head in that direction. The other officer looked apologetic as he backed out of the door, answering the radio that was pinned to his uniform. A couple of minutes later he stepped back into the room and made a gesture toward his partner. Officer Mitchell placed her hand on Rebecca's shoulder.

"Are you sure there's no one I can call for you? We must get going, but I can get someone for you, if you'd like?"

"No, really, I'll be okay," Rebecca insisted, while inside her head she was screaming that no, she wouldn't be okay, she would never be okay again.

Rebecca had no idea how much time had passed before she finally stood up. The police had left a while ago, but she wasn't sure how long she had been sitting there, staring off into space. Finally, she collapsed facedown onto the sofa, an animal-like wail coming from deep in her throat. The initial shock had worn off slightly and the pain hit her with the force of a train.

"Natalie!" she wailed, her fingers clawing the fabric of the sofa. It had been just she and her sister for so long, she couldn't even begin to wrap her head around the idea that she was alone. That Natalie no longer existed. Their parents, each the only child of older parents, had died years before, leaving the sisters with only each other for family. It was this bond that ensured that no matter how different they were, they remained in each other's lives and were a source of strength and support for each other. They were all they had. Until now.

Suddenly, Rebecca sat up straight. What had happened? Her sister was a healthy woman, and she hadn't been sick. The officer said she was found in her house, didn't she? That would mean it wasn't a car accident. So what on earth had happened?

Chapter Three

Detective Briggs ran his hands through his nonexistent hair as he walked through the precinct doors. Julie, the girl at the front reception, smiled and waved to him and he nodded in acknowledgment. It had been a long morning, but he had finally been able to turn the case over to Cranston and wrap up the survey of the yard. Someone on his team had also talked to every neighbor within a one-block radius.

He mumbled a curse under his breath and entered his office. He had moved to Spenser because he had grown jaded and tired of the crime in the big city. He had seen his share of cruelty, tragedy, and dead bodies. At 45 years old, he had hoped he would be able to cruise through to retirement working on cases of theft under $5,000 from backyard sheds, kids stunting in Daddy's car, and apprehending the local drunk trying to drive home under the influence. In the five years since he had relocated his wife Rita and his two boys, he had grown used to not looking death in the face. Until today. Even though it was a double suicide, it didn't make the tragedy any easier to handle. Sometimes, he thought, people are crueler to themselves than others.

He had begun doing the paperwork on the case when his newest deputy, Matt Adobenz popped his head around the door and came into his office.

"Hey Art, I have something I think you'll wanna see," he said excitedly. They didn't stand on ceremony here at the Spenser police station. What was the point of titles and formality when you knew you were going to be seeing your co-workers at church on Sunday and the person who reported to you might very well be your son's football coach?

He followed Matt to his desk and pulled up a spare chair and sat down. Matt tapped away at his keyboard, all the while talking a mile a minute.

"You mentioned the woman that was found this morning was a YouTuber, so I got curious. I watch some creators but didn't know we had one in town. So, I did a couple of searches on YouTube and bang, there she was!" Matt said triumphantly as he turned his monitor towards Art.

There was a photo banner along the top of yellow crime-scene style tape with text on it that read *For Crime's Sake*. On the bottom left side of the banner was a round profile picture of a beautiful woman with thick flowing auburn colored hair that Art recognized as the dead woman.

"That's her YouTube thing?" Art asked, a bit confused as to why it had made Matt so excited.

"Yup, and do you want to watch the last video she made and pinned to the top?"

"I don't know, do I?"

"Yes, you definitely do Art," Matt said with a grin as he clicked on the video and started watching it.

The video came up with a slick intro that included swirling crime scene tape that settled into the same configuration as the tape in the banner, heralding the name of the channel *For Crime's Sake*. After the intro, two people appeared on the screen. It was Natalie and a man, both sitting side by side and facing the camera. It began with her speaking, introducing herself as Natalie Baker and her guest as Peter Sogart.

"Holy shit," Art muttered to himself as he realized the man was the male corpse found at Natalie's house. These were the two people involved in the double suicide.

"Oh, just wait!" Matt said gleefully. The video continued with Natalie thanking her viewers for their ongoing support of her and her channel. She couldn't have done it without them. It was also through them that she had met Peter, who was her soul mate. They had met through this channel and quickly fell in love. They realized they both struggled with making sense of a world which contained so much evil and together they had decided it was not a world they wanted to live in any longer.

Art wouldn't have been surprised if someone had told him that his jaw had hit the floor. Not only did they have a suicide note, but they also had a live and in-the-flesh video testimony of their intentions. It was as good as tied up with a bow.

The video went on for a while longer with Peter talking about his love for Natalie and his depression and pain at the darkness he saw all around him. She held his hand and gazed lovingly at him as he spoke. The video lasted less than five minutes. At the end of it, the couple said their farewells and asked their viewers to please go forward and do something positive for someone else today.

The video ended with a closing sequence and Matt turned to Art. "I assume that's the male that was found dead with her?"

"Sure looks like him, although the last time I saw him, the shape of his head was a bit different," Art said rather sardonically. Dark humor was a trademark of professions that had to confront horrible realities every day. It was something Art hadn't shaken off from his previous job.

"Well, I better let the ME know we probably have an identity for the male," Art said as he stood up. "Good work Matt, thanks."

He had begun to walk away when something struck him and he turned around "Hey, do you think you could find out who Peter's next of kin is?"

"Sure, that should be pretty easy," Matt reassured him.

Chapter Four

Rebecca turned toward the table in front of the sofa, frantically looking for the business card Officer Mitchell had left. She grabbed it and found her phone.

"Spenser Police Station, can I help you?" the voice at the other end asked.

"Yes, can I speak to a..." she quickly glanced down at the card. "Detective Arthur Briggs?"

"Of course, one moment please."

It seemed as though the easy-listening music poured out of the phone for a long time before it was picked up again.

"Sheriff Briggs," the voice said.

"Sheriff Briggs, my name is Rebecca Robertson, my sister is Natalie Baker, and I was told to contact you for more information," she spoke quickly, the words pouring out of her.

"Hello Ms. Robertson, yes, I'm the person you want to speak to," Art said in the calm voice he had perfected when speaking to grieving families over the years.

"Okay, yes, the officer said you found my sister this morning in her house, what happened? How did she die? Why?"

"I'm sorry for your loss Ms. Robertson. Yes, I was in charge this morning. We found your sister after someone grew concerned. They had been scheduled to drop something off at your sister's house and she didn't answer." He omitted the fact that the person had glanced in the front window and had witnessed the tragedy inside. "I'm afraid your sister was involved in a suicide along with another person."

"WHAT?" Rebecca almost screamed. "Suicide? No, that isn't true, that can't be right!"

"I'm sorry, but it is," Art said calmly. He was used to family members responding in disbelief to news of the demise of a loved one. "There was a note as well as a video left behind."

There was silence at the other end of the line as Rebecca digested the information. Art was quiet and gave her some time before asking her if she planned on coming down to see her sister and wrap up her affairs.

"Yes, of course," Rebecca answered, although she sounded like she hadn't really heard what he was asking. Her mind was somewhere else.

"Okay, when you arrive, just come to the police station and I can help you with some of the things you'll need to do," Art said calmly. "Do you know when you'll be arriving?"

"Today," she stated firmly. "I'm on my way today."

As she threw random clothes into her suitcase a small voice was telling her she wasn't thinking this through. She was operating on autopilot, with her body moving of its own volition. She forced herself to sit on the side of their king-sized bed and take a deep breath. She needed to think things through. She couldn't focus on Natalie right now; she needed to plan her next steps. She would need to go to Spenser and identify her sister, then she would have to make funeral arrangements. After that, she would have to decide what to do with her sister's house.

It was a cute little home and Natalie had been so proud when she bought it. It was what she called a fixer-upper. She had done a bunch of work on it already and had plans to restore it back to its original glory. She didn't want to consider what she would do with the house right now; it was too painful. It was easier to focus on dealing with what was right in front of her.

She got up and grabbed a pen and notepad from beside her bed. She kept them there in case something was making her anxious.

Writing down a to-do list at two a.m. often helped to put the worry out of her mind, and she was then able to sleep soundly.

She started a list that began with filling her car up with gas and packing her birth certificate as she wasn't sure what type of identification they would need to prove she was Natalie's sister. She followed that up with a list of toiletry items and clothes. Almost as an after-thought, she added 'phone Jason' to the list.

She needed to phone her husband and let him know what had happened. Now that she had a chance to think things through, she realized he would want to be with her and help her. It was ridiculous to think that he would be more concerned with work. Shock was a strange thing and made people think such odd things.

She picked up the phone that sat beside their bed. Punching in her husband's work number, she waited for it to ring through.

"Hello, Jason Robertson's office, can I help you?" Tracy, her husband's assistant, asked in a perky voice that belied her usually dour expression. Tracy was a cross between a prison matron and the maid on the Brady Bunch, an old 70s sitcom. It was an odd combination of sternness and reliability.

"Hi Tracy, sorry to bother you, but I was wondering if I could please speak with Jason?"

"Oh, hi Rebecca, I'm sorry but Jason's in a meeting right now, can I leave a message with him?"

It took Rebecca a moment to process what Tracy had said and work through what she should do. She hated to bother him, but her rational side told her this was an appropriate time to interrupt him.

"Can you please get him anyway? It's very urgent," Rebecca finally said. Tracy must have heard the shock and uncertainty in her voice because she didn't question her or balk at interrupting Jason's meeting. Rebecca was not one of those wives who called their husbands constantly. If she said it was urgent, then it was urgent.

"Hello, Becky? What's wrong? I was in a meeting," Jason answered a few moments later. His voice was a combination of concern and annoyance.

"Jason, it's Nat..." Rebecca found the words catching in her throat. She hadn't said the words out loud and somehow, she felt as though saying them now made the whole thing more real.

"What about Natalie?" Jason probed.

"She's, she's dead," Rebecca managed to push the words through her teeth.

"Holy shit," Jason responded, one of the few times Rebecca had ever heard him swear.

She sat at the other end of the phone, clutching it in her right hand, taking deep breaths so she wouldn't break down on Jason. He was at work, and this was a shock for him too.

"What happened?" he finally asked.

"I don't really know, they say it was suicide," she whispered. "But there's no way she would do that, it makes no sense!" She felt her voice beginning to rise and she forced herself to stop talking so she didn't become hysterical.

"Well, we never know what's going on in someone's mind, do we?" Jason said logically.

A protestation arose in her throat, but she clamped down on it. She knew her sister better than Jason and she knew there was no way she would take her own life. It just didn't make any sense. Her sister was optimistic and loved life. She had suffered some anxiety in her younger years but had worked through that and was now living a life that brought her joy and happiness.

"What do you want me to do for you?" Jason asked quietly.

"I need you to come to Spenser with me to identify her and make arrangements," she blurted out before she had a chance to think about it any further. She knew he was busy, but she was speaking from her heart, expressing her needs clearly.

"Oh, geez Becky, this is a really bad time..." Jason began.

"I know, I know, you don't have to," Rebecca interjected. She had spoken without thinking and she regretted putting him on the spot. "I just said it without thinking. I know you have that big deal coming up."

"Yeah, you know I would if I could," he said.

"No, no, it's okay, I understand completely," Rebecca cut him off. "I'm going to get ready and drive down, I'm not sure when I'll be back or how long it's going to take me."

"You take whatever time you need," Jason said. "Just keep me posted on what's happening, okay?"

They hung up and Rebecca gave herself no time to think as she went down the rest of her list and packed what she thought she might need. Spenser wasn't that far from her home, but she didn't want to worry about driving there and back on the same day. She would pack enough for a couple of days, just in case. This would leave her options open.

Chapter Five

The drive to Spenser seemed to take forever until Rebecca pulled up in front of the police station. Then it seemed to her that it had flown by way too fast. She sat in her car, looking at the front door. She would have to go through those doors and confront the horrifying reality of her sister's death. Any chance that there had been a mistake would be finally gone.

She wasn't sure how long she sat there, staring blindly at the building. Eventually, she noticed someone had come to the door and turned to stare at her. He appeared to be a young police officer. They probably didn't get many strangers at the station, Rebecca mused. In a town the size of Spenser everyone probably knew everybody else on sight.

This was the motivation she needed, and she found herself sliding out of her car and walking towards the front door. The young officer smiled at her and opened the door wider, so she entered before him. The lobby area was small and consisted of a couple of chairs pushed up against the wall and a scratched coffee table, strewn with out-of-date supermarket tabloids. There was a counter and behind it sat a pretty young lady who appeared barely eighteen. The girl had a name tag that said simply "Julie." Rebecca wondered if her last name was missing for security reasons or simply because everyone in town automatically knew who she was.

"Hi Julie," Rebecca began. "I was told I needed to see a Sheriff Arthur Briggs? My name is Rebecca Robertson, he knows I'm coming."

"Oh yes, of course," Julie's smile slipped off her face and she looked as solemn as a teenager who had not yet had life slap them in the face could look. It was obvious that in this sleepy little town, Julie would immediately know she was next of kin to the poor dead woman. It made her uncomfortable to realize that a stranger might very well know more about her sister's death than she currently did. Rebecca took a deep breath to steady her nerves and keep her face impassive. There was no point in falling apart before she even had the chance to speak with the Sheriff. She needed to keep it together if she was going to get the information she needed and leave.

Julie picked up the phone and punched a couple of numbers into it. "Ms. Robertson is here," she murmured in a low voice as if she worked in a library. "Okay, I will. Art... I mean Sheriff Briggs will be with you in a minute," Julie passed the message along. "If you want to sit, he won't be long."

"Okay, thank you," Rebecca sat in one of the chairs and picked up one of the tabloids. She had barely opened it when she felt a presence near her.

"Ms. Robertson? I'm Sheriff Briggs, but you can call me Art, everyone does."

Rebecca looked up and saw a middle-aged balding man with brown hair and a soft middle. He had wrinkles around his eyes and a deep pair of vertical lines between his brows that showed his propensity to frown. He wasn't frowning at her now, but his face held a somber, respectful look.

"Good evening...Art," she said, sticking out her hand to grasp his.

Art had no doubt this was the victim's sister as they shared the same luxurious auburn hair and green eyes. The shape of their faces were similar, with Natalie's being rather narrower. This sister was paler, with freckles highlighted across her face. Art suspected that her pallor had more to do with the circumstances than anything else. He led her to his office and closed the door behind her so they would have some privacy when he shared with her the information he had been able to gather about the death of her sister. These types of conversations were never easy; giving the particulars of a loved one's violent demise inevitably caused incredible pain.

Before Art could begin, Rebecca began to talk. "I know what you said on the phone about it being a suicide, but I know my sister and there is absolutely no way she took her own life. I would like to know how she died and what makes you think it was suicide?" Rebecca pulled up a spare chair to his table as she spoke.

Art groaned inwardly. She wasn't going to make this easy for him. He suspected he would have to go through every small and potentially gory detail to convince her that her sister had died by her own hand. It was always a combination of heartbreaking and frustrating when faced with disbelieving family members. It was hard to watch them struggle to come to terms with how their loved ones died but it was equally frustrating when they refused to see what was so obvious.

"First of all, let me please share my condolences for your loss," Art said.

"Thank you," Rebecca responded in a clipped tone that implied she wasn't interested in pleasantries.

"We were alerted to a concern regarding your sister's home when someone phoned the station at eight this morning. They were there to drop off some paperwork for your sister. She didn't answer the door and the person was confused as they had just made arrangements two days ago for him to stop by on his way through town. He looked through the front window and saw your sister and another person lying on the floor. That is when they phoned us."

Art took a moment to gauge the expression on Rebecca's face. She continued to look stoic and resolute, so he continued. "When we arrived, we entered through the front door and confirmed that both were deceased. We then began to process the scene."

"And what made you think it was a suicide pact? Could it not have been a murder-suicide? Who was with her? Maybe they killed her and then themselves?"

"We know it was suicide because it was a pact and there was a note left by them both," Art continued. "In addition, your sister posted a video to her YouTube channel."

"May I please see the note?" Rebecca asked. She had begun to rub her left hand between her right thumb and index finger in a way that Art recognized as self-soothing. She was cool as a cucumber on the outside, but she was working hard at keeping it together.

"Of course, I have it here," Art pushed the note, still in the evidence bag, across his desk towards her.

Rebecca picked up the plastic bag and began to read the note. At one point, she swallowed hard and appeared to be struggling. Finally, she closed her eyes and let the note rest in her lap.

"Who is this Peter person? I've never heard of him," she finally spoke up.

"From what we've been able to figure out, he was your sister's boyfriend," Art answered. "Had she never mentioned him?"

"No, never. My sister and I were very close, I would have known if she was seeing anyone. I was always bugging her about needing someone in her life and she said she was fine being alone," Rebecca's eyebrows came together and she increased rubbing her left hand.

Art kept quiet, although he was thinking that we never really knew another person and maybe the closeness she felt with her older sister was more one-sided than she realized. It certainly wouldn't be the first time someone had concealed information about their lives from their family. "Do you want to watch the video she posted?" he asked.

"It's on her channel? I'll watch it later, by myself if you don't mind," Rebecca said.

"Of course," Art said, secretly relieved not to be around when she watched the video. This was one tightly wound woman, and he wasn't sure he wanted to be around when she finally let her guard down.

"Is there any paperwork or anything you need from me?" Rebecca asked. "Do you need me to sign anything or..."

"I don't need anything at this point, no,"

"When can I... I mean... where is... who has..." Rebecca floundered trying to put into words what she wanted to ask but Art knew what she needed.

"Your sister is at the coroner's office right now," Art said gently.

"Can I see her?"

"I'm sure you can, although I'm not sure if it would be best right now," Art didn't want to explain that they were still conducting the autopsy. Although it was obvious what the cause of death was, it was police policy to perform an autopsy to make sure there wasn't anything else going on. "How long will you be in town? I'm sure you could see her tomorrow."

"I'll stay as long as I need to," Rebecca responded. "Is there a place in town that you would recommend?"

"Well, there's only one place," Art smiled using one side of his mouth. "It's the Easy Eight, you'd have to have passed it on your way into town."

"Okay, I'll be checking in there then," Rebecca said. "If you have a piece of paper, I'll leave you my cell phone number in case something comes up."

Chapter Six

S he was grateful she had brought along her toiletries and some clothes, so she wasn't panicked about spending the night in Spenser. After renting a room for the night, she stripped down and stepped under a hot stream of water in the shower. She lathered up with her favorite body wash and inhaled the scent of grapefruit and pomegranates deeply. While she hadn't received much more information than she already had before leaving home, she felt like she was in the right place, and she no longer felt a driving need to be closer. Closer to what, she wasn't sure, although she suspected it was closer to her sister. A small sob escaped her, and in a moment, there was a torrent of tears falling down her cheeks. She began to sob, her shoulders shaking. Soon she dropped to her knees in the bathtub as the water poured over her and she curled up into a ball. She wasn't sure how long she sat there, sobbing and calling out for her sister but eventually her tears began to dry up and the water to cool.

She pulled herself out of the tub and dried off with the scratchy, thin towel provided by the motel. The place was clean and looked respectable which was what counted to Rebecca, but no one would mistake it for luxury. She slipped into her pajamas and crawled into bed. The TV was an old model that did not have the ability to browse the internet, so she grabbed her tablet and plugged it in beside her cell on the nightstand.

She quickly found her sister's channel and inhaled deeply to steel herself as she found the pinned video entitled "Crime's Sake Goodbye."

The thumbnail for the video had a picture of an old TV set with a blank screen and its electrical cord laying unplugged alongside.

She would rather be just about anywhere in the entire world than here doing this right now. But she knew she had to. She clicked on the link and watched her sister's video begin.

She gasped out loud as her sister's face filled the screen. She quickly tapped the pause button, so her sister's face was frozen in place. She looked into the face of her beloved sister, her hair falling along her shoulders, shining in the light. Her porcelain skin, with just a light smattering of freckles across the bridge of her nose. Her deep green eyes sparkled. Rebecca knew she looked like her sister, but she also knew she was like a photocopy; not quite as sharp and clear as the original. She was like a washed-out, less attractive version of her sister. Growing up she had resented the fact that her sister was the darling at home and with their teachers. But over the years, that resentment had receded as she watched Natalie grow into a kind and compassionate woman who wanted nothing more than to help other people. Over the years she had grown to respect and look up to her sister. They were two very different people. Rebecca was much more buttoned-down, organized and some might even consider a bit OCD whereas her sister was freer, cared less what people thought about her and more about what made her happy and what made the world a better place.

She tapped the video, so it began again, and she heard Natalie thanking her viewers and introducing Peter. Once again Rebecca stopped the video. She looked at the face of the man who had supposedly been her sister's boyfriend. He was average looking; his hair was beginning to thin and there was nothing about him that looked exceptional in any way. In fact, she suspected that many people would never even notice him if he was in a crowd. Or if they did, they would quickly forget him.

She frowned, not quite being able to reconcile her sister being in love with him. The video continued as they talked about their difficulty with living in a world that made no sense and that they didn't want to live in it any longer. Rebecca was watching the video when she realized she was shaking her head. No, Natalie, please stop talking, this makes no sense. This can't be true.

By the end of the video, tears were streaming down her face again. How could this be possible? When she last talked to her sister, Natalie had been happy and upbeat. She was talking about the cases she was researching for her True Crime YouTube channel. She was excited about the growth in her subscriber numbers and talked about a potential sponsor she was in talks with.

She hadn't mentioned this Peter and she wasn't depressed, of that, she was positive. Her sister was open with her when they talked, she wouldn't have hidden something as important as a deep depression or unhappiness with life.

She started the video again and watched it from start to finish without stopping this time. She felt as though her stomach was clenching and unclenching as a growing unease grew within her. This wasn't her sister. She knew it was crazy and that the evidence was right in front of her, but she couldn't help how she felt. This person was simply not her sister. While her eyes were strained and probably more than a little red, she knew what she had been watching and it wasn't Natalie. She rested her head in her hands and took a deep, cleansing breath. It was time to leave this and get some rest.

The next morning, she woke up with the sun and a throbbing headache. The tears and emotions from the previous day and night had taken their toll and she felt like a limp dishrag. She had hours to spare before anyone was in their office. She had checked with the phone book in her motel room — after she got over her shock that one existed — and found the number and address for the coroner's office. Now, she sipped hot black coffee made in the small pot in her room.

She was sitting at the table under the window of her room. The powder whitener floated in tiny clumps in her coffee, eventually clinging to the side of her cup. Occasionally, she took her finger and squished a clump up against the side in order to mix it in. When the other occupants of the motel began to walk by her front window she realized that time had passed, and she might be able to get a hold of someone at the Medical Examiner's office by now.

The phone was answered by the ME, and they agreed that Rebecca could come over right away.

MICHAEL CRANSTON HATED meeting with family members. Doing autopsies required him to approach the subject as an interesting puzzle to solve, a series of tests and dissections. Meeting the family only served to bring him face to face with the fact that he was working with a real person who had a life and people who loved them. He thought about this as he prepared Natalie Baker for her sister's visit. He draped her in such a way that her sister would be spared some of the more gruesome details of her death. It wasn't easy considering a 9 mm had blown a whole the size of a quarter out of her skull.

When Rebecca arrived, he was relieved to see that she appeared to be in control and wasn't going to pass out or melt into a sobbing puddle. He wasn't the best with other people's emotions. His husband teased him that is why Michael had become a Medical Examiner instead of a medical doctor who worked with live patients. He couldn't disagree; dealing with intense emotions from other people for a prolonged period would not be his thing.

"Come this way Ms. Robertson," he ushered her into his small, messy office. "I'm not sure what the Sheriff has told you about your sister's death?"

"He said he felt it was a suicide and that she had been shot," Rebecca answered.

The fact she said that the Sheriff felt it was a suicide rather than saying it was one did not go unnoticed by Cranston.

"That is correct, and I also want to make sure you understand that you are not required to see your sister for the purposes of identification. Between her fingerprints, the fact she was found in her home, and our ability to make a visual ID, your identification is not a legal necessity."

"I understand,"

"Okay, I also want to make sure you understand that your sister sustained head injuries which have distorted her appearance. Of course, I have draped her in such a way that if you choose to see her, you will be spared the worst of it." Cranston explained carefully. "Do you understand what I am saying Ms. Robertson?"

"You want to make sure I understand the fact that my sister was shot in the head will make her appearance unsettling, but you have done your best to hide the gore."

Cranston smiled slightly, pleased he was dealing with someone who was strong and didn't pull their punches.

"That is exactly what I mean," he responded.

"I need to see my sister," she stated emphatically.

"Then come this way please," he said, opening his office door and leading her down the short hallway toward a closed door.

Rebecca mentally gathered herself as she walked into the room behind him. As much as she hated the idea of seeing her sister's body dead and lifeless, she knew she had to do it. She needed to see her for herself, to make sure it was her, to truly understand that she was gone.

Michael Cranston approached a gurney, walking around to the other side and indicating that Rebecca should stand opposite him. He placed his hands on the sheet that was covering her sister, looking at Rebecca with a questioning glance until she nodded for him to go ahead.

Nothing could truly have prepared her for what she saw. It was her sister, her beautiful, vivacious sister. Lying cold and almost waxen, her skin had a bluish tinge. She reached out and gently touched her sister's cheek, feeling the coldness under her fingers.

"Would you like a moment?" Cranston asked.

"Yes, please" Rebecca whispered. Then they were alone. Rebecca swallowed against the lump in her throat. "Oh Nat," she whispered. "What happened?"

She gently moved a strand of hair off her older sister's face.

"I'm so sorry I wasn't there for you when you needed me," she continued. "I just don't understand."

She gazed at her sister's face, realizing that the closure she had hoped this would give her was not going to happen. Somehow, she thought that actually seeing her sister would help everything make sense. But it didn't. Natalie couldn't tell her what had happened because this was no longer Nat. It was a shell her sister had left behind. She wiped away the tears that rolled down her cheek. She had hoped she had cried herself out. Once again, she was wrong.

She leaned down and touched her lips to her sister's ice-cold cheek and said goodbye.

Chapter Seven

S itting in the parking lot of the medical examiner's office, Rebecca leaned her back against the headrest of the driver's seat. She was in a daze and wasn't sure what to do now. The medical examiner had told her that her sister's body would be released by the end of the day. She would have to contact a funeral home and make arrangements for them to pick her up.

From discussions they had in the past, Rebecca knew her sister would want to be cremated. This made it easier to decide what to do and she was grateful for their conversations around the topic of death. It wasn't something most sisters their age talked about, but when they had lost both their parents within a short period of time, it only seemed natural to talk about what they would want when their time came. Because she would be cremated, there was no rush to plan for a funeral or celebration of life. She could plan it and make those decisions at her own pace once she figured out what made the most sense. Right now, her mind was in turmoil, and she was afraid of making too many hasty decisions.

At that moment it struck her. There was no way her sister had taken her own life. She didn't care what the letter or the video said, it made absolutely no sense. It was as though her sister was sitting next to her in the car, speaking the truth to her and she knew with even more certainty that she was right. She knew her sister and she knew there is no way she would have suddenly taken her own life. And there was also no way she had been so seriously involved with someone and not told Rebecca.

She felt a certainty about this that she would never be able to explain to anyone else; she had to get to the bottom of what happened to her sister.

REBECCA DROVE AROUND Spenser, looking at the houses, and driving past shops that she knew her sister would have frequented, the coffee shop, the bookstore, and the grocery store. She wanted to get better acquainted with this town her sister had loved so much. When she first purchased her home, Rebecca had helped her move in and spent the night. But from then on, it was always Natalie coming to visit Rebecca whenever they saw each other face to face. It was amazing, she thought, that with the technology available to them, they spent so much time together yet apart. They video-chatted once or twice a week and exchanged online messages inbetween.

Before she realized what she was doing, she had swung her car into a vacant parking spot. She was parked in front of the bookstore. Entering the shop, she looked around with interest. It was an independent store and had the scent of old books but also a display of the most recent bestsellers. Natalie must have loved it. She poked around in the piles of books and walked up and down the aisle. The teenager behind the counter was looking at her curiously, her eyes following

Rebecca's every move. It was beginning to make her uncomfortable, so she picked up one of the cheaper journals from the stationery section and brought it to the counter.

"Is that everything?" the girl with the Brittany name tag asked.

"Yes, it is, thank you," she replied.

"Um, if you don't mind me asking, are you related to that Youtuber Natalie Baker?"

"Why yes, I am, she's my sister," Rebecca smiled at her, suddenly realizing why the girl had been staring at her so intently.

"I thought so, you look very similar," she said. "I'm so sorry to hear about her, she was real nice."

For a moment, Rebecca felt as though she had been hit in the solar plexus. For just a moment she had forgotten. She was so used to people commenting on their likeness and it brought back those old times when the clerk pointed it out. It filled her with a sense of familiarity that left a sharp pain in its wake. People wouldn't be making those comments for long. There would come a time when she would age but Natalie would remain the same youthful woman. Natalie would fade from people's minds. They would cease to notice that Rebecca looked like someone else.

"Thanks," Rebecca managed to whisper before grabbing her purchase and fleeing out the door.

Sitting in her car, she bent over the steering wheel and sobbed. The pain ran so deep, she couldn't imagine ever feeling normal again. How was she going to get through the rest of her life without her sister? Who would she talk to every week and tell all about the minutiae of her day? Jason was rarely available for a casual conversation; when he was there, she had a list of important things to ask him about and she didn't waste his time on things like how, as the years went by, it was becoming more and more difficult to keep the extra couple pounds off. Or an in-depth discussion about interior decorating and what colors would withstand the test of time versus which ones were just trendy this year. And what about holidays? How would she handle a Christmas without Nat? They usually spent the day in childless solidarity, sipping mimosas and roasting a crispy turkey while Jason complained about having too much work to do.

After a while, she was able to gather herself and head back to the motel. She had enough of being around people and was ready to hibernate for a while. The first thing she would do was pull out her laptop and do some research and how to handle Nat's estate. She assumed she had no will, at least none that they had discussed. Once all of that was settled, she would have to figure out what to do with her house and all her possessions. It suddenly dawned on Rebecca that she would probably be responsible for cleaning up her sister's house, after... what had happened. She assumed it was her responsibility, but how was she going to get through this?

She grabbed her cell and placed a call to the Sheriff's office.

"Hi, Sheriff, I'm wondering if you could tell me when my sister's house will be released?"

"It already has been, we've done all we need to do there," Sheriff Briggs answered. "Do you have a key?"

"Yes, I do. Can you recommend a cleaning company? I mean, like a forensic one?" Rebecca wasn't sure what to call the people who cleaned up in situations such as this one.

"Don't worry, I took it upon myself to have someone come in late last night. I hope it's okay, as I will have to send you the bill for it, but her insurance should cover it."

"No problem at all, I truly appreciate you taking care of that for me." For the first time in about 24 hours Rebecca felt a positive emotion, one of gratitude.

"Well, that is one thing about a small town, we try to look out for each other," he said. "No one should have to worry about something like that when they are grieving."

"Well, thank you again Sheriff, that's a load off my mind." She hung up and breathed a sigh of relief. She could go to her sister's house and not have to worry about what she would find there. It suddenly seemed very important that she be at the house, to somehow be closer to Nat.

She turned her car around in the middle of the quiet street, moving away from the motel and toward her sister's street. She drove north down the Hiawatha Pioneer Trail and turned off at 12th Street West. She drove as though on autopilot. Although she had only been there once, it was as though she heard her sister calling her.

Chapter Eight

S oon she was parked in front of the little 1940s wartime house that was her sister's home. It was a small unassuming home, reminiscent of hundreds of thousands of similar-styled homes across the US and Canada. The front window had been replaced with a small bay window and a fresh coat of white paint. It was located on a large piece of land and surrounded by towering trees and shrubs. Down the left side of the home was a driveway that led to an older garage that according to Nat was only good for keeping the snow off her car.

At first, Rebecca was confused as to why Natalie had chosen to move to Spenser, but while helping her move, she had come to see the allure of the town for her quiet sister. There were mature trees and large yards and the small older-styled homes like hers were mixed in with larger more expensive ones, including some enormous Greek revivals. The effect was one of a quiet, comfortable, and accepting neighborhood.

THE FRONT DOOR WAS an old metal screen door that banged when she opened it and the noise seemed to reverberate throughout the neighborhood. She could almost feel the neighbor's eyes on her as they looked out their windows to see who was at Nat's home. She slid the key into the single lock and stepped into the hallway that divided the home from front to back. On the right- hand side was Nat's living room and studio for taping her shows. On the left, was what Natalie had referred to as a conservatory. She smiled slightly as she leaned against the doorjamb and recalled teasing her sister about calling it a conservatory. Rebecca asked her if she was too famous a YouTuber to have a sunroom, or a lanai. But she knew this was Nat's favorite place in the home. She had a long, old-fashioned mid-century sofa against the long wall that faced the big window. There were plants all around the room and a tall reading lamp hanging over the couch. The walls were white, and the furniture was what Nat had called Tiffany blue. It was her favorite color. A fluffy white blanket was tossed over the armrest and cushions were piled in the opposite corner. In one corner was a built-in cabinet with glass doors. She had collected white and blue teacups and plates and displayed them here, where she could appreciate them from her couch. She always told Rebecca that she loved the old cups, and the more cracks and nicks on them the better. She liked to sprawl out on her couch and imagine the lives they had seen, the tea that was sipped out of them while women of a bygone era shared their heartbreak and the local gossip.

There was a small wicker table that was designed to slide under the edge of the sofa and act as a table. This was where her sister usually kept the novel she was reading. Rebecca bent down and picked up the novel, its pages folded back to keep track of her reading. Rebecca smiled at the title: Murder, Madness and Mayhem by Mike Browne. It was so quintessentially Nat. She was beautiful and vibrant yet had a love of all things dark and dead. Regret washed over her.

Why hadn't she come to visit? To sit here with her sister, in silence. Enjoying the presence of each other without the need for words.

"I'm sorry Nat," she whispered quietly.

THE REST OF THE HOUSE consisted of a washroom, a bedroom, kitchen, and living room. While certainly not a large house, it was perfect for Nat who had often referred to it as 'the cottage.' Looking through it, Rebecca decided to leave the living room for last. She

needed to brace herself before walking into the same room her sister
had died. She looked into the bedroom with its rumpled top cover,
pulled up in a rather pathetic nod to bed making and the toiletries
which were on the new granite countertop in the bathroom. It was
one of the first rooms Natalie had tackled after she bought the house.
She had had it gutted and fresh new white fixtures installed. The walls
were tiled in white with just a hint of grey and there were small pieces
of stained glass set into the updated window. Natalie had wanted to
renovate but retain elements of the antique and vintage items as a nod
to its origins.

The kitchen however, was more than just a nod to the past — it
was properly antiquated. The cost of doing the renovations she wanted
meant that it would be a while before the kitchen was touched. White
appliances, dark cabinets that appeared to be a type of stained plywood,
cracked brown tiles and a scratched stainless-steel sink adorned the
room. While Nat had always cursed this room, she had done so with a
hint of excitement as she considered its possibilities.

Finally, Rebecca walked through the archway of the dining room
into the living room. She stood there and looked around. Immediately
to her left was a beautiful woodburning rock fireplace that Natalie had
painted grey. It was flanked on each side with a white built-in bookcase
that was overflowing with books. In front of one of the bookcases was
a comfortable looking leather recliner in a butter cream color. On the
right side of the room was a long desk with two desktop computers, a
laptop, several ring lights, and a large microphone. At least it looked
large to Rebecca. She had always been amazed at how much her sister
knew about technology and how far she had come in the quality of her
videos. On the wall opposite the desk hung two floating shelves. One
had an over-sized magnifying glass propped up against some books.
The other shelf had a small fake plant with three more books. Rebecca
knew from her conversations with Natalie that she had installed strip
LED lighting along the back of each shelf to highlight them when she

was filming. On the floor off to the side, there was a large potted silk plant. The wall that ran perpendicular to the wall holding the shelves had a custom-made neon sign that said simply "Be the change." In the corner was a light on a tripod. This is where Nat spent most of her time researching and then taping her videos.

Up to this point, Rebecca had avoided looking down but now that she had been through the entire home, her eyes had nowhere else to go but to the center of the floor where her sister had taken her last breath. She wasn't sure what she expected to see, but when all that met her eyes was the worn hardwood floor that looked the same as the flooring in the rest of the house; she expelled a sigh of relief.

There was no sign of the violence that had occurred there, or whatever it was that had happened here the night before last. Once more she felt an immense sense of gratitude toward Sheriff Briggs. She sat down heavily in Nat's office chair and closed her eyes. It wasn't until she had faced this last mountain that she realized just how tense and strung out she had been. Her muscles relaxed and she leaned back further in the chair, tilting it back somewhat and resting her head on its back.

The next thing Rebecca knew, she was opening her eyes to a room whose shadows had lengthened and whose corners had darkened. She wasn't sure how much she had slept, but she was amazed she had been able to fall asleep so easily in this room. Swiveling around in the chair, she pushed the power button on the main computer and waited for it to load. She didn't hesitate to type 'Becky1987!' when it requested a password. For as long as she could remember, they had defaulted to the shortened version of each other's names and their birthdate when they needed a password.

She stared at the desktop for a moment or two before opening the web browser. She didn't feel right about poking around in Nat's files just yet. It felt invasive and way too soon. Instead, she decided to go through her sister's videos. Although she had watched all the ones on her sister's channel, some had been from a year or two ago and she needed the reassurance of her sister right now.

Chapter Nine

For the next few hours, she watched video after video. At some point she had changed the viewing speed to 1.5x so she could watch them faster while still being able to understand what was being said. She was about three-quarters of the way through all the videos when she realized it was pitch black outside and her eyes felt dry and scratchy. She couldn't believe it when she looked down at the computer's clock and realized it was 11 p.m. Thank goodness she had checked out of the motel room when she left this morning, or she would have to drive home in the dark. As it was, she had decided she would stay in her sister's house. If she could fall asleep in the same room as her sister had died, surely, she could sleep in her bed.

Before going in search of something to eat, she pulled out her cell phone to see if Jason had texted her. She had forgotten last night, and she was feeling bad for neglecting him. There was no message, so she sent one saying she was going to stay for a couple of days to deal with her sister's house. She hoped everything was going well at home and to please let her know if he needed anything.

Except for days when Rebecca was called in to substitute for an absent teacher, Jason was used to her being around and being able to make him a last-minute lunch, press a shirt or run an errand. Maybe it would be good for him to make do without her for a few days, she mused.

In the kitchen, she toasted a couple of pieces of bread, spread some peanut butter and jam, and poured herself a glass of milk. It wasn't a very original choice for comfort food, but she couldn't help it. It was the food that she and Nat turned to when they needed emotional sustenance. She took the sandwich and the glass of milk back to the desk and continued to watch her sister's videos.

It was comforting to watch her sister, so alive and vibrant, her gorgeous hair glowing under the lights, her light laughter tinkling out from the speakers. Rebecca knew without a doubt that these videos would be ones she would treasure and watch for years to come.

As she came closer and closer to the last video, Rebecca couldn't help but notice that at no time did she mention Peter or appear depressed in any way. There were a couple of times when she mentioned that she was skipping a video because she needed to take a mental health break as the work could get to her sometimes, but nothing that would have alarmed anyone. She had thought that she might notice something different now that she was re-watching these with fresh eyes. She had watched the videos within about a week of them first being posted, but now she watched with a more critical, piercing eye. Was there something she had missed the first time around? But there was nothing so far. Natalie had covered a string of long-solved murders that each had a particularly gruesome element or an unusual situation of some kind. Then she had begun to cover cold cases, going through the details of each case carefully where it was clear she had done a lot of research. Each video ended with Natalie saying something nice about the victim, attempting to humanize them and drive home the fact that this wasn't just an unsolved case, this was a person who was loved and loved in return. They had lived and breathed and contributed to this world, the same as we had. She then left contact details for the viewers if they had any information about the unsolved crime.

The last couple of videos were particularly heart-rending as they involved missing children. Rebecca knew her sister had a soft spot for kids and that these must have been difficult ones for her to do. Could that have been what threw her into such despair? That didn't make much sense since these were not child murders but cases about missing children. While the odds were probably in favor of them no longer being alive, these stories weren't the same kind of gruesome murders she had covered before. The more she looked around her sister's home and the more videos she watched, the less she believed it was suicide. She didn't know what had happened, but Natalie's home had fresh groceries, and there were notes for her next video. This was not the home of someone who was planning on taking their lives in a violent and horrific manner.

Chapter Ten

Rebecca grabbed the journal she had purchased earlier and a pen off her sister's desk. She needed to look at this like a puzzle; to lay out all the pieces and see if any fit.

She jotted down the facts of her sister's death; how she was found, the suicide note, how long they had been dead, and...Peter. Peter. Who was this man and how was he involved? Was he dating her sister? She added giant question marks around his name and began to go over and over them until her pen almost ripped through the paper.

It was time to do something she had been avoiding since she stepped foot in the house. She reached out for her sister's cell phone and decided the easiest way to get past feeling as though she was doing something she shouldn't was to just do it. She began looking through her incoming text messages, looking for Peter's name or some kind of communication with him. She scanned the files in the phone's camera but could only find pictures of sunsets, a couple of flowers, and some labels of things Nat had wanted to buy at the hardware store. She and Natalie had often discussed how hard it must have been for people to do things without a camera always at hand. They used it for things like taking a picture of your favorite brand of peas so you could make sure and get the right kind when you were next in the grocery store, or a photo of a light fixture cover so you could find a matching one. But there were no pictures of a man named Peter. In fact, there were no pictures of any men. There were no individual pictures of men and no men in a selfie with Natalie. How could Nat have had someone so vitally important in her life yet with no record of him anywhere?

FOR CRIME'S SAKE: WHEN TRUE CRIME KILLS 41

She reached over and jiggled the computer mouse and typed 'Peter' into the computer's search bar. There were three that came up in the downloads file. They were named Peter1, Peter2 and Peter3 and all three were videos. She clicked on the first one and a video began playing. It was the man named Peter. He was talking into the camera and seemed a bit awkward as he began. He talked about how much he had enjoyed chatting with her the night before and how he really hoped they could do it again. He mentioned how much they had in common and how beautiful she was. It didn't last long, but it left Rebecca feeling unsettled. Although he had mentioned Natalie by name, she was struggling to connect the video to her sister.

She clicked on Peter2 and watched as another video of Peter began. This time he was obviously more at ease and sure of himself. The last month or so, he said, was the happiest he had been in years, in fact maybe forever. She was everything he had ever dreamt of in a woman, but he never thought someone like her could love someone like him. She was a princess; a goddess and he didn't deserve her.

"Princess? Goddess?" Rebecca mumbled to herself. He obviously had not seen her armpit fart the national anthem.

The third video was more serious. In this one, Peter almost looked like he had been crying. He was definitely emotional. From what Rebecca could tell, they had had a conversation the night before about something that had disturbed him. "I understand what you meant; I really did. It's just so hard to wrap my head around it when we have only just found each other," he said quietly. "Think about it some more my love, let's not make any rash decisions."

What was he talking about? When was this video made? She right clicked on the file and then chose 'info.' The date it was created was nine days ago. Just over a week before they died.

Could he have been talking about a double suicide? But that would mean it was Natalie's idea. She couldn't imagine her sister agreeing to it, let alone being the one to suggest and talk someone into it.

She realized then that she had been thinking of Peter as some crazed person who had broken into Natalie's home and killed her after forcing her to sign the note and make the video. At that thought she clicked through to her sister's channel and played the goodbye message.

She had been avoiding it, but she couldn't any longer. If she was going to figure out what happened to her sister, she would have to face up to every little bit of evidence and information that existed.

After watching the short video where her sister thanked her subscribers and said goodbye, Rebecca sat at the desk, staring at the screen. Something was very, very wrong. She should have been devastated by this video and convinced of the scenario the police believed. There was something very wrong with that tape. Because she didn't know Peter, she couldn't comment on his appearance, but she knew that something was off about her sister. There was a blankness to her eyes as though she wasn't quite human. The light in her eyes wasn't there, there was no vibrancy and life that made up Natalie. She was surer than ever that something wasn't right.

THE COMMENTS UNDER her sister's goodbye video almost broke her heart all over again. The outpouring of love and concern from her subscribers was heartwarming and tragic. So many people had looked up to her and adored her. Many seemed devastated and questioned their own place in the world. Some were angry and lashed out at her for taking the easy way and leaving them to deal with things. She just couldn't imagine her sister not realizing the effect her death would have on her loyal followers.

Looking at her watch, Rebecca realized it was already two in the morning. She should get to bed and try to rest. It had been a very long and emotionally draining couple of days. At some point during the evening, she had made up her mind to stay and look into things a bit more before making the decision to head home. She would poke around and see if she could find out anything more about Peter and what his role was in her sister's life.

It took her about half an hour to make sure the house was locked up for the night and to prepare for bed. She was so exhausted that she was surprised to find herself lying in bed, staring up at the ceiling a good hour after going to bed. The room smelled like her sister and for some reason she hadn't expected that, and it was causing more emotions to bubble to the surface. Sleep eluded her and she tossed and turned. Finally, around three-thirty in the morning, she got up, plugged her earbuds into her phone, and turned on a playlist of her sister's cold case videos. Perhaps she would be able to fall asleep to her sister's voice.

Chapter Eleven

"What happened? None of this makes any sense, someone out there has to know something!" Rebecca sat up straight in bed, her heart pounding and her sister's voice ringing in her ears. It took her a moment to wake up enough to realize the sound was coming from her earbuds and her sister was wrapping up one of her cold cases videos.

The sun was streaming through a slit in the curtain and falling across her face. She must have slept through the night with her sister's videos playing in her ears. She decided to swing by the Sheriff's office. Now that she had processed things a bit better, she had some questions.

She ordered her coffee and was hanging around when the girl behind the counter spoke up. "Are you related to that YouTuber girl, Natalie?"

"I'm her sister," Rebecca answered.

"Yeah, sorry to hear about your sister, she was real nice," the girl commented. "She came in here lots to have a coffee and work on some of her research."

"Did she? Was she always alone?"

"Yeah, she was always alone and really into her work, if you know what I mean."

"I certainly do," Rebecca answered with a smile. She knew how engrossed Natalie could become when working on one of her cases. "So, she never came in with a man or met someone here?" She knew she wasn't being exactly subtle with her questioning but questioning people and trying to find clues was not exactly her forte.

"No, she was always alone," the girl answered, a small frown forming between her brows. "Is it true, you know, that a guy was with her?"

"Yes, someone named Peter," she answered quietly.

"Oh, yeah no. There was no one named Peter," the girl said.

Rebecca grabbed her coffee as soon as it was ready and left the coffee shop, grateful she didn't have to continue the conversation.

So, Peter wasn't part of her daily routine. They hadn't been together every minute of every day, hanging out together and becoming part of each other's lives, at least if his absence during her coffee time was any indication.

She was still nursing her coffee as she pulled up in front of the police station. She kicked herself for not bringing something for the Sheriff. It never hurt to be extra nice to someone from whom you wanted to obtain information.

After waiting a couple of minutes for Sheriff Briggs to become available, she was ushered into his office.

"Good morning Ms. Robertson," he greeted her.

"Please, call me Rebecca,"

"As long as you call me Art," he responded with a smile.

"Okay Art," Rebecca said. "I wanted to check and see if you had identified the man named Peter that was found with my sister."

"Yes, we have Rebecca, his name was Peter Sogart and he lived about an hour and a half outside of Spenser," Art told her. "We have notified his mother who is his only next of kin." "You mentioned that you had videos that proved it was a suicide pact," Rebecca said. "I found three videos on my sister's computer from Peter, are those the ones you meant?"

"Yes, at that point those were the ones we meant, but now that we have identified him, we have gone through his computer and found some that she sent him as well, videos that talk about their plans."

"I see," Rebecca said. She waited a moment, gathering her thoughts before asking "can I see those videos please?"

"Do you really think it will help or hurt you, Rebecca?"

"I think that whether it hurts or not, I need to know everything and I need to understand what happened to my sister," Rebecca told him, a note of steel in her voice.

Art picked up the phone and began talking to someone named Matt.

"Can you find a way to get those videos you found on Peter Sogart's computer to Natalie's sister Rebecca?" he asked. "Okay, yup, sure."

He hung up the phone and turned to her.

"Apparently he can email me a link that I can then forward to you. This will give you access to the videos," he told her.

"Okay, perfect. Is there anything I shouldn't be doing with these videos or any precautions I should be taking?" she asked.

Art looked confused and asked her what she meant.

"Well, I don't want to share it somewhere or say anything about it that might hinder the investigation," she elaborated.

Art looked at her across the desk, taking in her capable and shoot-from-the hip personality. He knew it was best if he was straight with her.

"Rebecca, there is no investigation," he said gently. "Your sister's death has been ruled part of a double suicide so the case is closed."

He looked into her eyes as he delivered this news, knowing that being as upfront as possible was the only way some people were able to digest information. Leave any room for ambiguity and they will leap on it as a reason to hope. He had expected to see devastation, sadness, or even anger in her eyes but what he was not prepared for was steely resolve.

"I know my sister did not kill herself, Sheriff and I am going to prove it."

Chapter Twelve

S he had gone through almost every video twice, scouring them for clues. For some hint of depression or some mention of Peter. It was at the point where she would have been surprised if she had found something. Rebecca was now on the cold cases; those cases that were old but still unsolved.

One of the videos was about a missing baby by the name of Sarah Jane Montgomery. It was a longer video than Natalie's channel usually made, and it had a large number of views. After grabbing a snack, she sat down and was quickly engrossed in the story her sister was telling.

It began four years ago in a town in the middle of Iowa, at a daycare that many locals used. It was run by a hometown woman and her husband, Sherrilyn, and Jim. It was the type of town where everyone knew almost everyone else. Many had grown up together and graduated from the local school system. Once Sherrilyn and Jim graduated, they went off to the big city where he took post-secondary in business, and she studied early childhood development. When they returned, they established a daycare center; Sherrilyn took care of the kids, and Jim took care of the business side of things. The video showed Sherrilyn and Jim in their graduation photos, at their homecoming, and on the opening day of their daycare center. They were smiling up into the camera, pride, and excitement evident on their faces.

The next series of photos were of the daycare itself, with Sherrilyn playing on the floor with the children, preparing meals, and rocking babies. Rebecca smiled a little as she realized how good her sister was at setting a tone and eliciting emotions. By watching this segment of the video, you would never know that Natalie wasn't crazy about children. It wasn't that she disliked kids, but she was preferred it if they kept their distance. As she explained to someone once "I'm just not the type to squeal when a newborn is carried into the room."

In fact, Natalie was pretty sure she wasn't going to have any children herself. This was the complete opposite of Rebecca, who had been aching for a child of her own for quite some time. She was waiting for Jason to feel ready, and he said he would be ready once his career was established. He had been working on that for a couple of years now. She tried not to think too much about when he would be happy enough in his career to start paying attention to the rest of his life.

Tearing herself away from these thoughts, she resumed watching the video. Natalie went on to say that Sarah Jane Montgomery was only nine months old and had been placed in the daycare when she was six months so her mother could return to her job. She was a happy, bubbly little girl with wispy blonde hair and cherubic cheeks. Rebecca's heart clenched as she watched the photos play across the screen.

It was a lovely spring day when Sarah Jane went missing; the older children were out on a walk and the toddlers were in a gated area. Two workers, Aleia and Bailey, had the toddlers under their care. Bailey was playing with them, and Aleia was rocking a stroller back and forth. The stroller held the sleeping Sarah Jane. The hood for the stroller had been pulled up and Sarah Jane was sprawled out on her stomach. The stroller was an old-fashioned one that they kept for just such occasions. It was too clumsy to take out for walks but acted as a perfect portable crib.

They had been outside for about fifteen minutes when Aleia asked Bailey if she could keep an eye on Sarah Jane as Aleia needed to use the bathroom. Bailey nodded yes and made her way over to the stroller. She sat down and proceeded to rock Sarah Jane back and forth gently.

When Aleia returned, she and Bailey stood talking, passing the time while their charges played happily. At some point, Aleia offered to gather the other kids if Bailey would take Sarah Jane into the daycare. It was while pushing the stroller into the daycare that something seemed off to Bea. She would later say she wasn't sure exactly what it was, but that maybe it was the lack of weight in the stroller as she pushed it and rocked it to get it over and through the threshold of the door.

Whatever it was, she looked down, moved the blankets around and realized there was no Sarah Jane. She screamed, Aleia came running and chaos broke out. Toddlers were crying as they picked up on the panic of the adults. Bailey was moving through the toddlers, double-checking that Sarah Jane had for some reason, and against all logic, gotten out and was playing with the others.

All the crying and noise alerted Jim who was in the office working on some paperwork. He came running out the door and into the gated area. After some incoherent exchanges he finally understood that one of the toddlers was missing. When he found out that no one had called 911, he frowned and shook his head in disgust while reaching for his cell.

The police arrived just as Sherrilyn and another worker returned with the older kids. But by then it was too late. Sarah Jane was never seen again.

Chapter Thirteen

In the ensuing investigation, the police split into two units. One was actively searching for Sarah Jane. They launched grid searches and hunted for her in all the databases of missing persons. If residents allowed it — and the overwhelming majority did — they searched houses, garages, sheds, and every ditch and hidey-hole they could find. The second police unit pulled apart the history and background of all involved. The first person they focused on was Bea. She was the last person to have possession of Sarah Jane and had only been employed by the daycare for a week. The young girl was distraught, and it took a while to get her to talk coherently. They looked into her past and found she was a local girl who had recently graduated from high school.

She was well-respected and liked by the other students and by her teachers. She was living with her parents until she could save enough money to move out on her own. In other words, there was nothing that indicated she could have had anything to do with the disappearance of Sarah Jane Montgomery.

They then turned their attention to Aleia, an employee of six months. She was not a local resident and had come to this town from another small town. She wanted to work at a daycare to gain experience and to decide if she wanted to go into a career that involved children. She was two years out of school but again there was nothing unusual in her background and the people in her town swore that she loved kids, had babysat many of theirs, and it was not within her to do anything to harm a child.

None of the other employees had a criminal record, as would have been expected in a situation where they were working daily with children. Jim and Sherrilyn did not appear to have anything hidden or nefarious in their backgrounds either. While they were local and the police officers themselves knew the couple, they investigated them just as they would have had they been unknown to them.

The police also investigated Sarah Jane Montgomery's parents. This was the first indication that something wasn't quite right. Apparently, there were rather heated arguments heard coming from their house that would often end with the sound of a slap or tears. The neighbors had called the police a couple of times but when they arrived, the couple swore up and down that it was just a disagreement and that there was nothing to be concerned about in their household. The police involved in the investigation were at first hopeful that this would lead somewhere but the couple each had clear-cut alibis. They were both at their work, about 30 minutes away, when Sarah Jane went missing.

It was at this point, Natalie explained, that the investigation came to an almost screeching halt. The search had turned up no sign of Sarah Jane. All those involved in her care had been cleared or at least the police had nothing that indicated a connection between them and Sarah Jane's disappearance.

Weeks went by, turning into months and finally years. Parents stopped bringing their children to the daycare and eventually it had to close. Jim and Sherrilyn moved out of town and out from under the cloud that followed them in their hometown. Shortly after their move, Sherrilyn was found dead in her living room by her husband. She had overdosed on prescription pills. While her husband protested that she wasn't depressed, everyone assumed she had harbored guilt over her role in the missing baby. Whether she had anything to do with Sarah Jane going missing, simply knowing that it had happened in her daycare and on her watch must have been devastating for her.

The staff of the daycare also dispersed and moved to other towns or cities. While none of them were suspects, they all were viewed with suspicion and it was just easier to move on than to deal with the side-eye looks and whispers. Within a year, Sarah Jane's parents divorced, and eventually, there was no one left to put pressure on the police and keep the investigation alive and on people's minds.

It was a sad story and for the first time, Rebecca began to wonder how her sister handled it all.

Chapter Fourteen

Natalie's channel, *For Crime's Sake*, ran a couple more videos of solved cases before she updated her readers on some digging she had done into the Montgomery case. She talked about how she had not been able to get this case off her mind and that she felt like Sarah Jane had been abandoned. There was really no one else out there that was actively searching for her or wanting to find out what happened.

After doing some more research, she discovered that Bea, the daycare worker that had discovered that the child was missing, had decided to get out of the childcare business. It was then that Natalie introduced a special guest to the channel. She would be referred to by her first name only as 'Bea.'

What followed was a compassionate interview conducted by Rebecca's sister. Bailey went over what happened that fateful day four years ago. She talked about how traumatic the whole experience had been for her and that it had changed her forever. She had gone back to school so she could get a better job in a totally different field. Rebecca asked her how it had changed her life, other than affecting her career choice.

"It changed something very deep inside me," Bailey explained, her eyes wet with unshed tears. "I no longer trust myself or anyone around me. In fact, I barely trust my sense of what is real and what isn't. I thought Sarah Jane was in that stroller and then she wasn't. It felt to me like she had literally disappeared into thin air. What I was so sure of one minute was proven utterly false the next."

There was a respectful silence before Natalie continued. "How does that play out in your day- to-day life?"

Bea smiled ruefully before answering. "I have what I would call borderline OCD. I mean I haven't been officially diagnosed, but I have to check my reality all the time. I might know I went to the grocery and bought milk, but then I find I have to go to the fridge just to make sure. It sounds silly, but I question my own reality at times." Natalie brought the interview to an end and then shared contact information if anyone knew anything about the disappearance of Sarah Jane Montgomery. A picture of the toddler was on the screen alongside a picture that had age progressed her by four years. The picture and contact information remained on the screen for a while and then slowly faded to black.

Rebecca sat back in the office chair and reflected on how she had never really thought about how much work her sister did for her job. She had liked to tease Natalie that she spent a couple of hours a week taping a video and then the rest of the time living like a lady of leisure. While she had known that wasn't true, this video brought back to her how much time, energy, and emotions her sister had invested in the work she did. It was no wonder she had such a loyal following. She was able to make a story come alive, and she went that extra step for her viewers. She was compassionate and had a way of creating videos that captivated and drew people in. The simple act of fading the picture of Sarah Jane to black was a good example.

Rebecca clicked on the playlist for Sarah Jane and began playing the next video in the series. This one included an interview with Sarah Jane's mother. It had a totally different feel to it than the interview with Bea. During this one Rebecca could tell that Natalie was struggling to connect with the woman who should have cared the most about finding out what happened to her daughter.

The woman seemed tense and almost defensive, as though she had been burned by the media in the past.

"I really don't know what I can add to this," she began when Natalie asked her to recount what happened that day. "I've told the police over and over again what happened. I've done many media interviews; I really don't know anything more than I have already said."

Natalie smiled encouragingly at her: "I know it must have been hard and you have been through so much, but by you telling your story, I'm hopeful it can draw attention to Sarah Jane's case and spark some activity."

"I was at work that day, there was nothing unusual about that day until I got a call from the police," the mother spoke as though by rote. "I couldn't believe what they were telling me, and I couldn't believe we were suspects."

The last part of her statement was said with a frown, as though four years later she still hadn't come to terms with how she was treated when her daughter went missing.

"We aren't using your new last name to protect your privacy," Natalie said. "But can you share with our viewers what life has been like for you since that day four years ago?"

"Well, my husband and I divorced a year later. It was partially due to the stress from Sarah Jane's abduction, but our marriage had been rocky for a while," the mother went on. "There was never any violence like people tried to make out, but it wasn't a very healthy relationship."

She paused and Natalie let the silence hang in the air. Damn she was good, thought Rebecca as the mother soon resumed talking without any further prodding.

"I moved away and met a wonderful man, and we married two years ago," she said quietly. "A year ago, I gave birth to two beautiful twin girls." The woman said the last part almost apologetically, as though she knew people would jump all over her. Natalie picked up on it too.

"Please know that you have nothing to feel bad about," Natalie said. "You have a right to go on with your life and find happiness."

The woman looked up at her a bit sardonically. "Well, yours is the minority opinion," she said bitterly.

"I'm sorry people have given you such a hard time," Natalie said quietly. Natalie's soft compassion seemed to open the floodgates and the mother began to talk more.

"It's just really frustrating. I mean it was my daughter who was taken, and then the police start treating you like a criminal, everyone stares at you when you go out in public, and even to this day there are people who think I did something to my daughter, even though I was miles away and have an alibi. I mean, I understand they had to look at us, but once we had an alibi, why weren't we treated like the victims we were? They certainly didn't come down as hard on that guy who was on the sex offender registry!"

"What guy?" Natalie picked up on it immediately.

"There was a guy in town who was on the sex registry for abusing young girls," the mother went on, her indignation opening her up enough to talk. "They interviewed him and then said he had an alibi and that was it. Why didn't we get that same treatment?"

"I didn't know anything about this guy," Natalie said. "Can you share his name with me offline? I'll see if the local police can shed some light on what that was all about."

"Of course," the mother said.

"Do you have any last words to leave the viewers?"

"Yes, when you hear a story in the media, don't jump to conclusions and judge people you've never met."

Natalie thanked her for her time. She turned to her audience and let them know that she had been trying to connect with Aleia, the worker who had been on the job for six months before and six months after Sarah Jane went missing but to no avail. If the viewers had any idea where she might be found, could they please contact her at the email address left in the show notes? She then ended the video with the same photos of a young Sarah Jane and an age-progressed one.

Chapter Fifteen

It was getting late in the afternoon and the sun had moved across the sky. Rebecca felt as though she had wasted a lot of time watching so many videos and not doing anything. But watching her sister do what she loved to do had a soothing effect on her. It took her mind off the horror of her sister's death, if only for a while.

But now it was time to start looking into what had happened to her sister. To begin with, who was Peter? She went to her phone and forwarded to her sister's email address, the videos the Sheriff found on Peter Sogart's computer.

Once they showed up in her sister's inbox on her desktop, she began watching them with a pen and paper nearby in case she needed to make a note of something. The first video took her breath away as she watched her sister come online. She was sitting exactly where Rebecca was right now, in the same chair, with the same background. She looked happy but a bit anxious. Like Peter's video on Natalie's computer, in this one, she referred to enjoying their conversation and how glad she was to have met him. She was excited about their future and how much good they would make in the world, together It was obvious this video had been made when she returned home after a date with Peter. The videos back and forth seemed to be their preferred way of communicating.

Rebecca had the same sensation as when she watched the goodbye video her sister and Peter had supposedly made. There was something she couldn't quite put her finger on — a lack of life and vibrancy that made her sister her sister. She hoped she wasn't imagining things because she so badly wanted to see something that told her the police were wrong and her sister had not taken her own life. But no, something was off, she knew it.

The second video made it obvious that their relationship had progressed quite a bit since the first video. Her sister talked about how she couldn't believe how she had found her soulmate after searching for so long. At this point, Rebecca paused the video and made a note on the paper beside the keyboard. Her sister didn't believe in soulmates and hadn't been looking for one.

Of course, a devil's advocate could say she was now in love and therefore spouting romantic drivel, but she made a note of it anyway. The video carried on in the same vein although at one point she said something that Rebecca found quite interesting. Natalie referred to the fact that it seemed Peter wanted to meet but that she wasn't ready. She stopped the video again. So, they had never met in person? This was an online relationship only? And why wasn't Natalie ready to meet him? The Sheriff mentioned he only lived an hour and a half away; it wouldn't have been that hard or even that much of a time investment to take the time to meet. Her sister had talked disparagingly about people who dated without ever meeting. She claimed no one could really know someone until they were close enough to smell each other. Rebecca jotted down another note.

The video ended with more of the same type of talk: love, longing, and patience seemed to be the theme of this one.

The third video showed a distracted Natalie, full of deep sighs and angst. She talked about how hard she was finding it to delve into the dark underbelly of human nature all for the sake of views. She wasn't sure how much more of this she could take before she was going to have to do something. At this point, Rebecca was scribbling wildly on the paper. There was no way this made sense. Natalie always told her how grateful she was that she lived in the time she did where she could research and broadcast her videos and hopefully help someone. On more than one occasion she had told Rebecca that she didn't care if she had only ten views on a video, if it was the right ten to help solve a case or provide comfort to someone looking for closure. This video made it sound like her sole purpose for her channel was to get views and make a living.

The video ended on this depressing note and Rebecca was almost afraid to watch the next one. In this last video she least resembled the Natalie Rebecca knew and loved. There was a decline in her sister's mental health and an almost cynical attitude toward everything. But she knew she had to watch them all, so she clicked on the final video.

She wasn't sure what she expected to see on the video but there was no way she could have prepared herself.

"I know it's hard Peter, I know this isn't easy, but we must do it. I've thought about it for a while now, and it's the only way. You know what the darkness is like more than anyone, and you also know it will keep coming back. I don't want this anymore and I need you to support me. I know we will be missing out on some things that I have looked forward to like growing old with you, becoming parents, and holding our baby, but it isn't enough anymore.

Come by tomorrow night, bring your gun and whatever I say, whatever I do, don't let me back out. You have to be the strong one here Peter, you must take care of me and make sure I don't hurt anymore. You're the only one who can help me. Then we can be together forever, and we don't have to deal with this shit anymore. The darkness will go away for good, for both of us."

Rebecca felt as though all her breath had left her body at once. There it was, the actual planning of their suicide that the police had referred to. She could understand why they thought it was an open and shut case. But what they didn't know was that this was not her sister. The look in her eyes, the comments about soulmates and children? This was *not* her Natalie.

Chapter Sixteen

Rebecca grabbed her cell and did a quick search on Peter Sogart. There wasn't much online, but an obituary had been posted this morning and she was able to find out his mother's name. After a bit of digging, she managed to find a number for Millie Sogart and she quickly punched the name in before she could lose her nerve. The idea of disturbing a woman who was grieving her son was not exactly something she was looking forward to.

The phone was answered on the second ring and Rebecca asked to speak with Millie. A moment later, the phone was picked up again and someone said, "Millie speaking." She was surprised at how old the woman sounded. While she hadn't given it much thought, she had pictured someone younger than this frail-sounding woman. Rebecca hesitated even more, unsure if she should intrude.

"Hello?" Millie asked.

"Hi! Hi Millie, you don't know me, but my name is Rebecca Robertson, Natalie Baker was my sister," she decided to just blurt it out rather than beat around the bush.

"Oh! Oh, I'm so glad you reached out!" Millie said.

"You are? I wasn't sure you would want to talk to me," Rebecca was surprised at her response. "I wasn't sure I should phone."

"Oh my, why ever not?" Millie protested, sounding surprised. "Any family of Natalie's is welcome to reach out any time."

"Thank you, that's very gracious of you," Rebecca said. "Would you by any chance be able to meet me?"

"Well, I don't drive anymore but I supposed I could get my neighbor to take me to visit you somewhere," Millie sounded uncertain.

"No, no, I can come to you," Rebecca didn't want to put the woman out or inconvenience her, she really did sound elderly. "What about tomorrow at about 1:30?"

"That would be lovely, my address is 1220 Glenwood Park in Cedar Falls, do you know where that is?" Millie asked.

"I can find it no problem, and thank you,"

She had some time to spare so she decided to switch her focus and look into the child abduction case. One of the areas she wanted to pursue was information on the sex offender that the mother had mentioned. Had he really been cleared or was there something that was missed? She did a search of the newspapers around that time and found several updates on the abduction. Most of the articles implored people to offer any assistance to the searchers that they were able to and explained how people could donate to the search for the missing little girl. But then, just as the articles began to become less frequent and interest in the case apparently waned, there was a small item in the local paper saying that local police were reporting that they had looked into every possible suspect, including any local sex offenders and all had verifiable alibis. She supposed that was going to have to be good enough because without some help from the Sheriff, this was all she had to go on.

REBECCA DECIDED TO give herself a break, so she pulled on her coat, grabbed her purse, and left the house. She would drive around until she saw a restaurant that appealed to her. She would probably just get something to go as she wasn't much up to facing people right now. And apparently, she looked enough like her sister that she wouldn't go unnoticed in this small town.

She wondered how Jason was doing while she was gone. It didn't seem to faze him that she wasn't around, but it had only been a couple of days. There had been times when she thought he wouldn't even notice if she wasn't around and so far, she hadn't been far off. He was so engrossed with his work and advancing his career that they rarely saw each other for more than an hour or so every day. She had talked to him about it a few times, but he kept reassuring her that it wasn't forever, just until he was secure in his work, until he had proven himself and was seen as indispensable. But in Rebecca's mind, that was an unrealistic goal because no one was irreplaceable when it came to work. There would always be someone who could do your job.

She pulled into a strip mall that had a pizza place with flashing lights running all around the large front window. This was just what she had in mind. Cheap, greasy food. But first, she fired off a text to Jason, touching base and letting him know she would be another couple of days at least.

Back at the house, she set the pizza box on the table and went in search of a glass for her soda and a paper napkin. She hadn't realized how hungry she was until she walked into the restaurant. The smell of baking pizza had hit her nostrils and she wouldn't have been surprised to discover she was salivating. None of this was surprising because she couldn't recall the last time she had a real meal. She had watched videos all day and missed lunch. She dug into the pizza and quickly ate a couple of slices before she talked herself into slowing down. The pizza was amazing, and she didn't think it was just because she was hungry either.

After she was done, she went back to Natalie's computer, but this time she did a search under "true crime" on YouTube. She wanted to see how other creators put together their videos. What she was surprised to discover was a community of people who watched many of the same channels, interacted with each other in the comments, and seemed very passionate about true crime. As she read through the comment sections, she realized that her sister was part of this community, in fact, many mentioned her and her last video. There was a sense of uncertainty among the viewers. Rebecca hadn't realized that for many who watched her channel, the last thing they heard from Natalie was what was in the last video, the goodbye one. Essentially, they had been left hanging.

She thought about it for a while and then her sister's voice came to her: "you can find whatever you need on YouTube or Google." Her sister had said that so often Rebecca had threatened to have a t-shirt made for her with that saying on it. She began typing into the YouTube search bar "how to make a video and upload it to YouTube." Just as her sister had predicted, a large number of videos came up. Luckily her sister's camera, mic, and lights were already set up well enough for her to bypass a bunch of the instructions. She tried taping a couple of clips to get the hang of where she needed to look, and how loudly she needed to speak. Then she wrote down a couple of points she wanted to remember, took a deep breath, and began.

When she awoke in the morning there were hundreds of comments on her video. Person after person expressed their condolences and talked about how much Natalie would be missed, and how much they loved her. There were also notifications showing her sister's channel was tagged and when she followed the links, she discovered that other YouTubers in the true crime community had posted videos and comments as a tribute to her sister.

She sat reading all the comments with tears streaming down her face. Her sister had been so important to so many people. She was not alone in her grief and somehow that helped and brought her some reassurance that her sister's life had not been in vain. She had touched many with her passion and her need to see justice done.

Soon she had to pull herself away from the computer and get ready to see Millie, Peter's mother. She was glad she had posted the video when she did as the comments had given her an infusion of energy and determination to keep going. Perhaps meeting with Millie could shed some light on her sister and Peter's relationship. It sounded like Millie may have met Natalie and if that was the case, it must have been very recent, and she might have some insight into their relationship.

Chapter Seventeen

When she pulled up in front of Millie's home, she sat for a moment and stared at the rather dilapidated home. Whereas Natalie's home was old and had a specific character that Natalie was working to bring out bit by bit, it was obvious that Millie's home had seen better days. From the road, Rebecca could already tell it was a house that was put together in a hurry and with cheap materials decades ago.

She wasn't sure what to expect as she rang the doorbell but even so she was surprised by the frail old lady that answered. She was petite and slightly hunched over with short wispy white hair growing from a delicately pink scalp. The hands that reached out to hug Rebecca were shaky and lined with blue veins. For a moment, she wondered if she had the right Millie Sogart, and if so whether she had misinterpreted Peter's age.

After letting her go from her hug, Millie ushered Rebecca into her living room.

"Can I get you some tea my dear?" Millie asked.

"No, I'm fine," Rebecca said, hoping she wasn't offending the woman but not wanting to put her out. Just then a cat leapt onto her lap and began to purr.

"Oh, Captain Kori," Millie admonished the cat. "Leave our guest alone, shoo! Shoo!" "Don't worry about it, there is nothing like a good cat snuggle once in a while," Rebecca laughed, scratching behind its ears.

"I can't disagree with you there, but once you start scratching one, you have to scratch them all," Millie said as she reached down and scooped Captain Kori up in her arms. Rebecca watched her as she took the cat out of the room. She then heard a door opened and quickly slammed close. The sound of protesting cats could still be heard with the door closed.

Oh my, Rebecca thought to herself, what had she gotten herself into?

"There we go, all set," Millie said as she shuffled back and sat on a chair in the living room. "They are great company until I get company!"

Rebecca smiled along with Millie and wondered how she could ask the questions she needed to ask without upsetting the old lady. Luckily, she didn't have to as Millie set the ball rolling herself.

"I'm so sorry about your sister, she was a lovely girl," Millie began. "My son loved her so and she made him so happy."

"So, you met my sister?" Rebecca asked, getting right to the point.

"Oh yes, my Peter introduced us, he met her oh, about a month or two ago I think it was. Well, at least that is when he told me, you know kids these days, they don't want us parents all up in their business."

Rebecca fought not to smile at Millie's use of the colloquial expression and for referring to her sister and Peter as children. She was pretty sure people in their thirties and forties could technically be referred to as "kids these days."

"Was Peter an only child?"

"Yes, he was and as you can probably tell, he was a late-in-life baby," Millie smiled, her eyes sheening over. "His father and I were so shocked when I learned I was expecting. We thought it was our lot in life not to be blessed with the patter of young feet. But my husband Charlie, God rest his soul, he stuck by me all those years when it was just us."

Wow, Rebecca thought to herself, that Charlie was one saint.

"Then boom! Along came Peter!" Millie suddenly exclaimed in a loud almost screeching voice that made Rebecca jump slightly. "And he was a beautiful baby, would you like to look at some

photos?" She was already reaching forward to the pile of photo albums on the coffee table and Rebecca knew she couldn't say no. For the next half hour or so, they sat together on the couch, flipping through page after page of a growing Peter. Contrary to what Millie had said, Peter was in fact not a very attractive baby. He looked squished up and mottled with a slightly misshapen head until he was a few months old. From there he grew into a somber toddler and a gangly schoolboy. Unfortunately for Peter, it was all downhill after that; by high school, he was scrawny and acne-ridden, and in every picture, he looked like he was trying to meld in with the background so as not to be noticed.

As Peter grew into a young man, the photos became less and less frequent as though he had finally put his foot down and said: no more pictures. The last one was of a thirty-something Peter, hair thinning, a slight paunch forming around his middle. While Rebecca was trying desperately not to make judgments until she had all the information on Peter and her sister's relationship, it was hard to think of her sister as finding this man attractive.

"That's it for the photos," Millie said sadly. "I guess I won't be having any more to add."

Rebecca reached out and held Millie's soft, thin hand. No matter what Rebecca thought, this woman had lost her only son and was clearly hurting.

"He was a lovely son, I'm sure you were very proud of him," Rebecca said quietly. "What was his occupation?"

"He was a security guard down at the salvage yard, he worked there once he was released from the hospital. I don't know if Natalie told you, but he spent some time there dealing with depression. That was why he moved in here, so he could be free of stress and make enough money to get back on his feet," Peter's Mom explained.

Rebecca wasn't sure how to tell her that Natalie had never mentioned her son, not even once.

"So, Peter brought Natalie here to meet you?"

"Oh, heavens no, he said they weren't at the stage of her coming to visit yet," Millie explained.

"So where and when did you meet her?" Rebecca looked at Millie quizzically.

"Well, they were chatting one night, and Peter asked me to come meet her," Millie looked pleased at the memory. "So, I went over to his computer and there she was, such a beautiful girl!"

"So, you never actually met her in person?" Rebecca probed, trying to understand what Millie was saying.

"No, but Peter said that these days you say you have met someone when you chat with them. He explained it's the same as meeting face to face, except you see each other over the computer."

Rebecca wasn't sure, but she thought maybe Millie thought she was a bit slow or maybe not "with it."

"Do you know how they met?" Rebecca changed the subject slightly. "That must have been online too?"

"Yes, it was," Millie's brow furrowed as she looked at her with some confusion. "Didn't Natalie tell you this?"

"No, we hadn't gotten into the details." A small white fib but she didn't want to hurt the woman by having her find out that Natalie hadn't even mentioned Peter to her family.

"Oh yes, of course. He was a fan of hers for a long time, he was always watching and rewatching those videos of hers. To be honest," at this Millie leaned forward conspiratorially "I never really understood why so many people were interested in such horrible goings-on. I told Peter a couple of times I didn't think it was good for his mindset but then she answered one of his comments and they started talking. He was a happy man and who was I to say that was a bad thing?"

"Of course not," So her beautiful, happy, and YouTube-famous sister reached out to Peter, one of her plain, mentally unstable fans who lived with his mother. Then, after never having met face to face they supposedly fell in love and planned a suicide pact. Why was she the only one who found this to stretch credibility?

"I'm sorry to have to ask you this Millie, but... were you surprised to hear that they were dead?"

Millie looked at her for a long time, as though choosing her words carefully.

"My dear child, since Peter was a teenager, I've been worried about this very thing happening. Throughout his struggles and when he was in the hospital, I had so many sleepless nights. So, was I surprised? The answer is complicated because I was surprised it happened at this time when he finally seemed so happy, but I have been waiting for this most of his life. I can honestly say that the only part of it that truly surprised me was that your sister went with him."

AFTER THEIR TALK, REBECCA sat in her car, staring at the steering wheel, unsure how to process what she had learned. Suddenly a thought struck her, and she left her car and went back up the walkway to Millie's door.

"I'm sorry to bother you again, but I was wondering if Peter might happen to have a laptop with his conversations with Natalie?"

"Yes, he did, but the police took it when they came to talk to me," Millie said, confusion evident on her face.

"I know this might sound crazy, but I think there is more to their deaths than the police say, and I was wanting to go through both my sister's and Peter's correspondence to see if anything stands out."

"Oh well, of course, I don't know what I would do with it anyway. Peter was the one who knew how to work it, I don't think I would even know how to turn it on," Millie said. "You are welcome to it when the police are finished. To be honest it will be one less thing for me to do."

"Okay, would you be able to phone the police station in Spenser and ask for Sheriff Briggs? Just let him know I can have it."

"Of course, dear, anything I can do to help."

Chapter Eighteen

The ride back to Spenser went by in a blur for Rebecca. She went over and over everything Peter's mother had told her about their relationship. It supported what she had seen in the videos so far, including Natalie not wanting to meet. But why? Why wouldn't she want to meet? Natalie was a take-charge kind of woman who liked to face things head-on. If she was truly involved with someone, she would want to meet them sooner rather than later. It was as though she was putting together a jigsaw puzzle where the pieces seemed to be the right size and shape to fit each other, but they didn't quite match.

She pulled up to the police station just before four and she hoped someone would be able to help her find out more about Peter's laptop. Julie smiled at her when she walked through the door, as though she had been expecting her. Going up to the counter, she began to tell her why she was there, but Julie put up a hand and spoke

"Don't worry, I know what you're here for, Sheriff Briggs left it here for you," she reached over on her side of the counter and pulled out a laptop that was in an evidence bag.

"Oh, they're done with it already?" Rebecca asked. She knew she shouldn't be surprised that the police were wrapping things up, but she was.

"Yup and Millie called to release it to you so if you can just sign here..." Julie pushed the paperwork over to Rebecca and she dutifully signed beside the 'x'.

"Thanks, Julie, I appreciate your help," Rebecca said, leaving the police station minutes after she had walked in. It had all happened so fast and so easily that she couldn't help but be surprised. She had anticipated having to wait for them to be finished with it and then have to jump through more administrative hoops to have it released to her rather than Millie, Peter's next of kin.

But not one to stop and question things, she backed out of the lot and headed toward her sister's home. As she approached the house, her heart began to beat faster, and she caught her breath.

"Oh no, no" Rebecca cried in a quiet voice as she stared in disbelief.

Chapter Nineteen

Natalie's dream home was marred by streaks of red and glass shards were lying in the grass around her front window. The window of her conservatory had a large, gaping hole in it and the word "death" was smeared in red paint across the glass.

She came to a screeching halt in front of the house and got out to look at it in dismay. "Oh, Natalie, I'm so, so sorry," she thought to herself. All the hours she put in under a hot sun scrubbing and painting the outside of the house had been ruined. Her conservatory was ruined. Who would be so cruel as to attack a dead woman's house like this? And why? It was at that point that the anger began to rise inside her. How dare they do this to her sister's dream? It wasn't bad enough that she was dead, but now someone was trying to ruin the only thing left of her. She reached for her cell and punched in the police department's number.

"Sheriff Briggs please," she told Julie when she answered. "I don't care if he is busy, please tell him it is important."

A few minutes later, an annoyed Sheriff was on the line.

"What is it?" he demanded.

"Sheriff Briggs, someone has vandalized my sister's home and you need to come out right away to see it, and to conduct a proper investigation," she said firmly. It was all she could do not to tell him that this should be a real investigation, unlike the one into her sister's death.

"I'm finishing up a meeting and then I will stop by on my way home," Sheriff Briggs said, in a voice that made it plain he would not jump just because she called him.

"Okay, should I wait outside in case the people who smashed the windows are inside?" Rebecca asked innocently.

"Oh Jesus, just sit still and I'll be there shortly. Don't touch anything."

She hung up the phone with a small sense of smugness that she had won this one. But seriously, what did he think she meant when she said vandalized? Threw some eggs? For all she knew they had made their way into the house and were waiting for her. Of course, she had no idea who "they" might be, but still.

She stood leaning up against her car, staring at the house. From what she could see, the conservatory window had been smashed on the lower left side. There was what appeared to be paint on the window, as well as across every wall and window she could see from the street.

How could this have happened in broad daylight, and no one saw anything? The word "death" had been painted across the conservatory window and the word "house" across the other side of the house. "Death House" How original, thought Rebecca. Was this a bunch of delinquent kids or was someone trying to send her a message? Was the death house reference to what had happened in the home or was it a threat of things to come?

But why would someone try to threaten her? As far as anyone knew, she was a grieving sister staying at the house to take care of her sister's estate. Except for the video she posted last night. The one where she announced her sister's death and ask for more information on cases she might have been working on. Was it possible that request had hit a nerve for someone?

She was caught up in her thoughts when the Sheriff pulled up in his squad car behind her vehicle. He slowly got out of his car and sauntered over to her. They stood side by side, facing the house.

"Well, someone made a mess of this," he said.

"Yah think?" Rebecca responded sharply.

"Well, let me check things out and make sure no one is inside," the Sheriff said as he walked up the sidewalk. "Stay here and wait for my say-so."

"No worries about that," Rebecca responded.

She watched as he walked around the house, taking in the vandalism and noting the shards of glass. A couple minutes later he walked back and asked her for her keys.

"I assume you don't want me to do more damage by kicking down the door?" he asked.

She looked at him with one eyebrow raised. It was obvious he was not taking her concerns very seriously.

He unlocked the front door and disappeared into the house. When he came out, he gestured for her to go on in.

"I'll call Frank, he's the only guy in town who will be able to help you out on such short notice. He'll either fix that window or secure it until he can get what he needs ordered," he informed her.

"Thank you, I appreciate that Sheriff," Rebecca said almost grudgingly as she wouldn't have had a clue where to look for help. "Do you know where I can find some reliable teenager who might be interested in a side job of slapping on a coat or two of white paint to try and cover this up?"

"Let me give it some thought, and I'll get back to you," he spoke with his back to her as he walked away. "Have a nice evening."

"Yeah, sure, you too," Rebecca mumbled under her breath. It appeared that now that he had made his decision about her sister's death and everything was tied up with a bow on it, he had little time or patience for her.

ALTHOUGH THE SHERIFF had gone through the house, Rebecca couldn't help but feel a bit edgy that night and she jumped at every little creak. She decided to do some poking around the house and see if she could find any sign of Peter having been in the house prior to their death. A t-shirt in the laundry hamper, a spare stick of deodorant in the bathroom, something. She was going through her sister's bedside table when she came upon a journal with her sister's scrawling handwriting inside.

She sat down on the bed and started reading the entries starting about two months ago. There weren't a lot of entries as Natalie was obviously not a dedicated journaler, but Rebecca reasoned that it would mean if she took the time to note it in her journal, it must be important.

She felt a bit voyeuristic as she read her sister's thoughts. Natalie was concerned about how to reach more people with her channel, and what project to take on next in the house. In one entry she wrote about a conversation she had with Rebecca. Her breath caught in her throat and for a moment she wondered if she should stop reading. Not only to protect her sister's privacy but also to protect herself. What if she wrote something that Rebecca didn't want to hear or couldn't deal with? What if she expressed a negative opinion of her?

Nevertheless, she plowed on, her heart had been broken into a million pieces when her sister died, she had a hard time imagining her sister saying anything that could hurt her even more. The entry was dated less than a month ago, after a conversation the two sisters had about possibly taking a vacation together.

"I don't know what to say to Rebecca when we have conversations like this. How do I get it across to her that she has to live her life and not wait for Jason? He is never going to change; he will always be dedicated to his job more than to her and she deserves so much more than that.

She doesn't want to go on a vacation without him, but he won't go until some far-off date when it is a good time for him. So, she doesn't go anywhere as she waits for him. It breaks my heart to watch her settle for this kind of marriage."

Rebecca gaped at the journal and its entry. Her sister had hinted at times that she wasn't the biggest fan of Jason, but she had never come out and expressed her displeasure with their relationship. Was it true? Did she wait around for Jason? Was her life on hold? Her mind immediately went to her desire for a child. She had been ready for years, but Jason kept saying the time wasn't right. And yes, if she was honest with herself, she had a hard time thinking that he would ever think it was the right time. She had turned down the vacation with her sister because Jason was busy at work, and as a result she had missed invaluable time with her sister and making memories that would have lasted a lifetime. Who knows, maybe her sister would have opened up with her about Peter and what was going on with her channel. Could things have been different if she had only agreed to go with Natalie?

She thought back to when she first introduced Natalie to Jason. Her sister had been lukewarm when they met and never really warmed to him. When Rebecca pushed her for an opinion, Natalie told her that while Jason seemed like a nice enough guy, she didn't see him as being a life partner for her sister. She explained that Jason was what Natalie called "dishwater soup." She meant that he was bland and rather unappealing. Rebecca had tried not to show how her comment hurt, but it stuck with her. Going forward, she only talked about Jason in glowing terms, reinforcing to her sister what a catch she had landed when she married him.

Apparently, she had not fooled Natalie at all. Because the truth was, if she was being honest with herself, Jason was exactly as Natalie had described him. He was a bit bland and rather boring. He was a plain-looking man who could enter a room and twenty minutes later people wouldn't recall having seen him. He certainly wasn't unattractive, he was just...there.

She shook her head to stop where her mind was taking her. She couldn't play these types of games that would only cause her pain. What had happened had happened and no looking back could change that now. And anyway, her marriage had nothing to do with what she was trying to do here; she needed to focus on finding out what happened to Natalie.

Chapter Twenty

Once she had confirmed that there was no mention of Peter in her journal, Rebeca opened Peter's laptop and began opening folders and searching for anything that might have to do with her sister. By the time she had gone through his desktop folders, she had discovered he was a big *Dungeons and Dragons* fan and enjoyed Sudoku.

She dug a little deeper into the computer and then did a search for her sister's name. She realized she should have done that first as several files quickly appeared. She sorted the files chronologically and began with the oldest file. There was an assortment of letters and videos that were from her sister to Peter. In them, she talked about her day, how her channel was doing and some of the cases she covered. It was apparent that in some of the correspondence, she was responding to something he had said, usually about them meeting in person. At one point, she mentioned the meeting with his mother and told him what a darling lady she was. The more recent ones became grimmer and more negative, with her reminding him about what it felt like to be in the darkness and how it was just going to keep happening over and over.

Rebecca set the letter to the side and leaned back in her desk chair. This was not the way her sister would have talked to a man who had a history of hospitalization due to depression. It was not the way anyone should talk and Natalie had to have known what a dangerous line she was walking. Why on earth would she tell him that his depression was only going to return time and time again? It made absolutely no sense.

She turned back to the letter and continued reading. Her sister continued to talk about how much evil there was in the world and how tired she was getting of it all. The next file that came up was a video and she watched her sister talk more about how hard life was becoming. Rebecca realized she was getting to the point where she could watch these videos and not see them as her sister Natalie. Despite what she was seeing with her eyes, her heart did not recognize this woman. At the end of the video, Natalie she said she needed to run because she had an appointment at three and it was already two.

Rebecca clicked on the online calendar her sister used and flipped to the day the video was created. There were reminders to phone the handyman for an estimate and another to set aside time to research the SJM case further. But no mention of an appointment at three or any other time that day or the day before or after. Was she just lying to Peter to cut it short?

Possibly, but it was more in keeping with her sister's personality to say she had to go and get some work done. Rebecca had certainly been at the receiving end of that comment many times during their phone or chat conversations. She just wasn't the type to lie for no good reason.

The next video referred to how glad she was to have some time to work on her next video as she had the whole day free for a change. Once again, she consulted her sister's calendar which indicated that Natalie had an appointment entered to interview Bailey regarding the SJM case. Why would she say she was free when she had an important interview? Again, it was explainable as a white lie, or maybe she meant the interview was part of her work on her next project; but why put it that way then? These comments were all beginning to add up and Rebecca felt like she was finally getting somewhere.

Just then, Rebecca heard a sharp knock on the front door. She froze, wondering who could possibly be coming to the house of a dead woman. She peeked through the peephole and shook her head at her silliness. It was what appeared to be a workman, probably here to fix the conservatory window. She opened the door wide.

"Hi there Miss, Sheriff sent me over, said you had a window issue," said the man wearing a hat that had "Frank's" written across the top in block letters. "I was going to ask you where the problem was but then I drove up and I think I can figure things out." He said the last bit with a rueful smile.

"Yes, I'm afraid the damage is pretty obvious," she said, opening the door for him to enter. "The room is right here." She took him into the conservatory with the broken glass lying on the floor. Rebecca hadn't realized he was coming so soon, or she would have swept up the glass in the room herself. As it was, she simply hadn't felt ready to tackle it. In addition to the broken window, the red paint scrawled across the window cast an eerie and sinister glow across the room. He reassured her that he would take care of the clean-up and she left him to his work.

As she walked back to the computer in the living room it struck Rebecca that in all the videos Natalie sent Peter she had been sitting here at her home studio. When the sisters chatted, Natalie would often do so with her phone and walk around the house doing chores or getting dinner ready. However, all these videos were only done in her studio. If she was so comfortable as to profess her love for this man, why was she concerned about keeping up appearances?

After watching it one more time, Rebecca turned off the last video where she talked about him coming to her house with a gun. She stared at the screen pensively, uncertain of what to do next. On a whim, she grabbed the mouse, opened the browser, and googled her sister's name.

There were a massive number of entries that popped up, many of them recent and about her death. She had scrolled through those and onto the next page of results when something grabbed her eye. It was a link that said, "Helping Natalie Baker aka *For Crime's Sake* on Sarah Jane case." The link was to a Reddit subpage. Rebecca was shocked to find post after post of people sharing thoughts and information on the disappearance of Sarah Jane Montgomery. The last couple of posts discussed the death of Natalie Baker, the YouTuber. Most of the posts were supportive, although there were a couple that the people interested in this case to give it up or that Natalie was obviously unstable. Rebecca continued scrolling through the posts; there were ones on the poster's opinion on who took Sarah Jane, and some reported the work they were doing on trying to find the second daycare worker. A lot of people had opinions on Sarah Jane's mother and how the interview with her went.

After reading for a while, she switched over from the browser to the search bar for the computer. Rebecca typed "Sarah Jane" into the bar and found a folder with that name on the hard drive. She was looking at the file names when she noticed there was a folder within the Sarah Jane folder. The folder was labeled "Wakefield". Inside was a document that contained links to various articles on a baby that had been abducted from a maternity ward. Apparently, the baby girl had a tracker on her umbilical cord, but the tracker was found in the empty bassinet which was located near an exit. There had been no sign of her since and the case had gone cold. There didn't appear to be any suspects, even though the police interviewed everyone on the floor that night and even the parents. One piece of information was highlighted in yellow and that was the part that mentioned that the father of the baby had a history of domestic violence. A comment had been made on the document that said, "significant or coincidence"?

Another folder was labeled "Sabbie" and inside it, there were links and articles that documented an abduction from a daycare center in Canada. The baby was six months old when it was taken from the center in a manner that eerily resembled Sarah Jane's abduction. Again, everyone from the workers to the owners of the daycare and the parents were thoroughly investigated but the baby was never seen again.

After combing through the two folders, she noticed that there was a video file entitled "Connection?" She double-clicked on it and a video of her sister popped up. This video was a rough cut without an introduction or any editing but it was clear what the topic was.

Her sister presented the information about the missing baby from the hospital and the six-month-old from the daycare. The one thing she added in the video was that the parents of the child missing from the daycare were receiving subsidized care since they had very little income after being discharged from prison.

As she watched the video, she was vaguely aware of Frank wandering in and out of the house as he brought supplies back and forth. He hummed quietly under his breath and she realized how nice it was to have another human in the house with her.

Near the end of the video, Natalie had taped a couple of endings. One was of Natalie looking into the video and saying "two babies, one set of parents suspected of domestic violence, the other ex-cons. When you hold these two cases up against Sarah Jane Montgomery's case, you begin to see more and more similarities. All three were girls, all three went missing without a trace while under the care of someone other than their parents, and all three had parents with some potential criminal activity in their backgrounds. Are they connected in some way?"

As the video came to an end, Rebecca became aware of someone looking over her shoulder. She whipped around in time to see Frank looking at the monitor with interest. He quickly backed away as though caught doing something he shouldn't.

"Okay Miss, I've blocked off the window so it's safe for now," he began explaining. "I'll have to order a piece of glass that will fit that window as it's pretty large and has to be custom-made."

Chapter Twenty-One

Rebecca watched through the front door as Frank gathered up his tools and loaded them onto his truck. She felt a sense of relief as she watched him drive away. She knew she was probably getting overly paranoid, but it had thrown her to catch Frank looking over her shoulder with so much interest. She knew realistically that he was probably just a nosy townsperson who wanted to have something to talk about with his cronies.

Trying to take her mind off things, she walked into the kitchen and made a sandwich for herself. She was thinking that it probably wasn't healthy to be so immersed in these videos, but she really needed something to go on. She found a piece of paper and a pen in the kitchen and began scribbling down all the things she had learned. Then she began another column listing all the things that just didn't add up. She had just finished the list when suddenly the house went quiet. Totally quiet. The usual background hums that you don't notice until they stop were no longer there. At the same time that it happened, she heard the computer in the living room beep. It had shut down.

"What the hell?" Rebecca asked herself. She opened the fridge door and sure enough, the light did not come on. The power was out, but why? She looked out the front window and didn't notice anything unusual on the street; no one came out to see what had happened or to talk to their neighbors, asking questions to see if they too had lost power. Rebecca called the operator and asked to be connected to whoever supplied power to Spenser. She sat tapping her fingers as she waited for more than twenty minutes. During that time, she noticed one of the neighbors come out and lock their alarm system behind them. There didn't seem to be a problem with their electricity.

Finally, after about half an hour, someone took Rebecca's call. She explained the power had gone off just after noon and she was wondering if there was a problem in the area. The customer service representative asked for her name and the house number. Rebecca explained that the house was her sister's but that she had recently passed away and that she was her sister. She crossed her fingers, hoping that they would still talk to her. Issues around privacy had sometimes become a major inconvenience.

The representative put her on hold again but came back after only five minutes this time.

"So, the home is in the name of Natalie Baker, from Spenser?" he asked.

"Yes, that is correct," Rebecca responded.

"There are no issues in the area, but your home was tagged to be shut off at noon today."

"What? Why would it be shut off? Were the bills not paid?" Rebecca knew her sister was diligent about paying her bills and she hadn't been dead long enough for a bill to be overlooked.

"The note on the account says someone called in and asked for the electricity to be turned off because the owner was deceased," he explained, reading the note out loud.

"Does it say who called?"

"Yes, it was a Rebecca Robertson."

She was struck silent as she took in what he had said. There was no way she had called. She needed the electricity and hadn't even begun to think about shutting the house up. Who on earth had called and shut it off?

"Ma'am?" the representative asked. "Do you want it to stay off or do you want it reconnected?"

"I absolutely want it reconnected," she said with certainty. "Don't you require some kind of identification or will or power of attorney or *something* to be able to just shut it off?"

Why would they just take someone's word for it that they were Rebecca? And why would that person shut down her power?

"Umm... I'm sorry but we do try to offer some loosening of our policy in the event of a death, we don't want to make things more difficult for the family."

Rebecca frowned and felt her heart rate increase. She had long forgotten her thoughts on the too-stringent rules companies had for identification these days. uneasiness began to rise in her and as she sat at the table, her phone perched on one shoulder, she wrote "Electricity" under the column of things that didn't make any sense.

Occasionally, Rebecca had bouts of insomnia, but for the most part she was a healthy sleeper. That night she spent most of the night staring at the ceiling. She was going over in her mind the cases in the Sarah Jane Montgomery file. The Wakefield baby and the Sabbie toddler. Were they connected in some way? and did that have anything to do with her sister's death? Had she maybe gotten too close to an answer and was killed because of it? But if so, how did Peter fit into things? Was he connected with the case somehow and was he the one who killed her to keep her quiet? But then why kill himself? No matter how many different ways she looked at it, she couldn't seem to find a way it made sense.

Chapter Twenty-Two

As the sun was beginning to rise and cast grey shadows around her sister's bedroom, Rebecca drifted off into sleep.

When she woke, a little past ten, she got ready and headed to the grocery store. She couldn't avoid the locals any longer, and she needed to get some food. After driving up and down some of the streets, she found a store. Beige vertical clapboard was topped by a large green sign that read Family Mart in white. She parked in the lot beside the store and headed in.

As soon as she entered, she knew it was going to be an uncomfortable shopping trip. Almost every eye within her vision was focused on her. People turned their heads when they saw their friends staring at her and then joined in.

She knew it was inevitable, as Spenser didn't exactly have a high crime rate. And a double death? That was big news. It was annoying and uncomfortable, but she knew why they were doing it. She grabbed a cart and went in search of sandwich meat, bread, cheese, and some frozen dinners. When she was at home, she cooked elaborate meals for Jason, but they often went cold before he had a chance to eat. But here, the pressure was off, and she could just look out for herself and not worry about anyone else. Her menu would be simple.

Once she had her few groceries in the cart, she held her head high and headed for the check-out. She smiled at the cashier and as she left, she wished her a good day. When she returned to her car and put the groceries away, she sat for a bit, waiting for her heart rate to lower and the emotions to roll over her. Being stared at only reminded her of why she was here. These people must have known Natalie, and she berated herself for not taking the opportunity to try and talk to them, maybe find out something she didn't know about her sister's life.

She put her car in drive and headed back to her sister's house. She took her time and went the long way home as she wanted to spend more time out of the house. As she was driving, she had the odd sense she was being watched. She glanced in her rear-view mirror for the second time and noticed the grey sedan was still following her. As she drove, the sedan turned the corner just before the house. She mumbled under her breath to get a grip on herself, it was just a local who lived in the same area. She shook off the unease and began unpacking the groceries. She was walking into the house when she heard her phone; she received about five texts one after another.

She set the bags on the kitchen counter and then checked her phone.

"I need to talk to you" her husband's first text said.

"As soon as you get this, call me."

"You've been gone too long and I need you here" "So call me"

"On my cell phone, I have a meeting to go to and I might be on my way," he ended the texts.

Well, if he was on his way to another meeting, it couldn't be life threatening she mused. Then she corrected herself: even life threatening might not be enough to tear Jason away from work.

She called him and the phone only rang once before Jason answered.

"I think you need to come home," he said immediately.

"Well, hello, and I miss you too honey," Rebecca joked. "What's the sudden rush, did you run out of frozen meals?" The words were out before she could think. But Jason didn't seem to notice as he continued talking.

"When I got home last night, I decided to check the mailbox, because you haven't been here to keep it empty, it was pretty jammed full." If she didn't know him better, she would have almost thought his voice was accusing. "There was a letter in it for me."

"Yes?"

"It said I'm supposed to tell you to mind your own business, or your sister won't be the last to die," he stated. "You need to come home now."

Rebecca was silent, thinking about this new turn of events.

"Why aren't you answering Becky? Say you are coming home," Jason insisted. He was used to her following his directions immediately.

"I'm thinking Jason, give me a minute," she snapped.

"Well, what is there to think about? If someone takes the time to send a threatening letter, I'm thinking we need to pay attention."

"But don't you wonder why they sent it in the first place? Why do they care that I am looking into my sister's death."

There was silence on the other end as Jason absorbed what she had said. Rebecca brought her palm to her head as she realized she had purposefully led him to believe she was just wrapping up her sister's estate.

"I don't know what you're doing there in the butt-crack of America Becky, but you need to leave it be and come home."

"Why don't you throw the letter in a courier package and I'll take a look at it," she said, trying to keep her voice calm and reasonable. "That way I can see for myself."

"What? you think I made this up to get you home?" he demanded.

"Of course, not Jason, you're being silly, I just want to see it for myself."

"Well, how am I supposed to courier it? I'm not around the house enough for them to come get it," he said, a slight pout to his voice.

"How about you ask the office to send it and you'll pay the cost?" It never ceased to amaze Rebecca how he could be climbing the corporate ladder but in the day-to-day things, she had to hold his hand and treat him more like her child.

"I suppose I could do that," he said reluctantly. "But once you get it, you'll come home, right? I can send it expedited."

Oh sure, now he was suddenly a courier expert, she thought with a grin.

"I'll probably come home," she said, her fingers crossed. "I just want to see it and figure out if it is a real threat."

They ended the phone call and Rebecca put the rest of the groceries away. She knew she should feel grateful that her husband was so concerned about her welfare, but instead it made her feel a bit claustrophobic. He never asked her what she thought, he just made demands, even in a situation like this one.

Chapter Twenty-Three

S he made herself a sandwich and went back into the living room to read the comments on the video she had posted. She was beginning to see how it could become addictive: post a video, watch people react. After a while she decided to get more active and start asking questions, just like she should have in the grocery store. Some of these people seemed to really know and understand her sister. She would start with Reddit where the activity seemed to be more active with regular contributors.

She signed up for an account and posted on her sister's sub-reddit.

"I'm Natalie Baker's sister and I'm looking for more information on some cases she was working on when she died. Has anyone been in contact with her about them?" She decided not to include the names of the cases so she would be able to tell if someone actually knew anything. She didn't know if she was way-off base, thinking the cases had something to do with her sister's death but at this point, she wasn't sure what other avenue to pursue. Heck, she wasn't even sure what she was looking for at this point.

She decided to place a call to Sheriff Briggs. She would check to see if he had found someone who could paint the house and at the same time, she would mention the threat.

"Hello Ms. Robertson," he said, obviously using his patient voice. "What can I do for you today?"

"Frank came over and patched the window and is ordering a new one," she said. "Thank you for that."

"No problem at all,"

"Um, did you happen to come up with any names of teenagers that might be interested in a paint job?"

"Yeah, my sister's boy is trying to round up a crew so they can knock it off quickly this coming weekend," he said. "I was going to contact you when they figured things out."

Well, Rebecca thought to herself, that would be what you would call someone's "don't call me, I'll call you" voice.

"Okay, thanks."

"You're welcome, is that all?"

"No, actually," Rebecca began. "My husband received a threatening letter in our mailbox telling me to stop looking into things or my sister might not be the last one to die."

"Okay, but don't you live in another state?" he asked, sounding confused. "What would that have to do with me?"

"I just thought you might like to know Sheriff." Now she was getting irritated at his obtuseness. "Don't you think it's strange for me to get a threatening letter mentioning my sister if she had in fact committed suicide?"

"Look, I don't know what you get up to in your regular life, I don't know what enemies you have or don't have, but that is something for your local police to look into. Get your husband to take it in to the station and show them," Sheriff Briggs said.

"Too late," she responded, quietly.

"Too late? What do you mean too late?"

"My husband has put it in a courier package and it's on its way to me now." For the second time that day Rebecca crossed her fingers. No point in telling him it probably hadn't been mailed yet. Jason wouldn't take the time to take it to the local police and even if they did, what could they do? They were trying to warn her off what she was doing in this state, not her hometown.

The silence on the other end lasted a while but Rebecca waited him out.

"Okay, fine bring it in when it arrives," the Sheriff finally said, exasperation evident in his voice.

"Thank you, Sheriff," she said as she hung up the phone. She felt just a slight sense of having won that round and frankly, she could use the encouragement. She refreshed the Reddit page and noticed there were several comments under her post. She ran down the comments, realizing that most of them, rather than providing an answer to her question, were expressing their condolences and telling Rebecca how much they would miss Natalie and what an amazing addition she had been to the true crime community. She was taken again by this world Natalie had created that was a part of her everyday life.

Later that afternoon, there was a knock at the door, and she wondered if Frank was back to install the new conservatory window. But it was a courier with a package for her. She was a bit surprised it had arrived so quickly and hated to think what Jason had to have paid to get it here so soon.

The courier envelope had a letter-sized white envelope inside. There was no address on the outside and it was sealed shut. She carefully pried it open and saw a slip of paper inside. Where was the original envelope it had arrived in? Was it just a slip of paper that had arrived at their house? She slid the contents out onto the desk and pulled each flap back carefully with a pen. She was no police officer, but she knew enough to try and not touch it. Sure enough, it was a note as Jason had relayed. Inside, it said simply:

"Tell your wife to mind her own business or her sister may not be the only one to die." It was typed out in a plain Arial font and was printed on simple copy paper. In other words, nothing unique or distinguishable at all. She folded the letter back up with the pen and awkwardly slipped it back into the white envelope. it was time to take it to Sheriff Briggs and see if there was anything he could do with it.

Before she pulled out onto the street, she fired off a text to Jason asking if it had come with an envelope and if so, where was it? She arrived at the police station five minutes later and bound up the steps. Julie smiled at her and before Rebecca could say anything she asked

"Sheriff Briggs?"

"Yes please, Julie," she answered with a smile. Oh, the joys of small-town life.

Julie answered her phone and then told Rebecca she could go on back to Sheriff Briggs's office. "He says you should know the way," Julie said.

She headed back and walked through the Sheriff's open office door.

Sheriff Briggs was sitting at his desk, clicking away on his computer. She stood there for a moment, eventually clearing her throat to get his attention. He slowly pulled his eyes away from the monitor and looked at her with both eyebrows raised in a question.

"I have the note, it arrived by expedited courier," Rebecca said, lifting the envelope to show him.

"Oh great," he responded, rather unconvincingly. "Pass it here then."

As she passed it to him, her phone dinged with a text. "The note is right inside, I was careful not to touch it," she told him as she looked through her purse for her phone. When she had located it, she checked her messages and Jason had sent one.

"There was an envelope, but I didn't keep it, didn't know I should."

She immediately texted back "did you touch it?"

"Of course, how else was I going to read it?"

She sighed with frustration. He had been so worried about her; he hadn't even thought things through properly. She looked up at the Sheriff who was now staring at her.

"I'm afraid my husband touched it and threw out the envelope," she told him.

"Look Ms. Robertson, I don't know what you want me to do with this. I could look for fingerprints but what for? We have nothing to compare them to and the person who sent them is probably from your state," he explained slowly. "If it's any consolation, it's probably one of those, what do they call them? Haters? Of your sister, I mean. Apparently, she was known on YouTube and that's going to attract the crazies."

Rebecca stood in front of him for a minute, looking down at him, expressionless. She was beyond frustrated with this man. It was like he was digging his heels in and refusing to acknowledge something was going on. Instead of leaving, Rebecca sat down.

"I want you to look at something Sheriff," she began, pulling out the list of things she had learned and the things that didn't make sense. "This is a list of things that don't add up, things that just don't fit."

Sheriff Briggs leaned back in his chair, rocking slightly as he looked at her. Finally, with a resigned sigh, he reached out for the list.

"Let's see, no doctor's appointment when she said she had one, appointments when she said she didn't, she didn't walk around the house when she filmed with him, she didn't want kids but told him she did..." his voice trailed off as he looked at the rest of the list. Finally, he handed the paper back to her. "Ms. Robertson, surely you can see how these things are small and easily explained? People say all kinds of things when they are in love, that doesn't mean there is anything nefarious going on."

"But..." she began.

"No," he cut her off. "No buts. Listen, I understand that you are grieving your sister, I truly do, but you need to deal with that grief in a constructive way instead of denying reality."

She stood and stared briefly at him before turning on her heel and walking out the door.

Chapter Twenty-Four

"Damn! damn! damn!" Rebecca was sitting in her car in the police parking lot, taking out her frustrations by pounding on her steering wheel. What would it take to get through to that man? Why would he not even consider what she was saying? He had just patted her on her head and told her to be a good little girl. She sat there for a while, alternating between pounding her steering wheel and letting out discreet little screeches so she didn't alarm people passing by her car going into the station.

She was just going to have to resign herself to the fact she was in this on her own. The Sheriff wasn't interested in helping and her husband didn't even ask how things were going because he just wanted her home. She was going to have to do this herself.

She drove back to the house, determined to keep digging and find out what on earth had happened to her sister.

THIS TIME SHE HIT PAYDIRT almost immediately after sitting down at her sister's desk. For some reason, she hadn't noticed a file in the bottom left-hand corner of the computer's desktop. It was called simply "stuff." When she opened the file, she realized these were notes and odds and

ends that her sister would jot down while she was working, and random thoughts came to her.

She scrolled down through Natalie's notes reminding her of appointments, ideas for videos, and two or three-word thoughts. Some of them made her smile, others made her scroll on quickly as she heard her sister's voice so clearly. She needed to stay focused on the task at hand. Near the end of the list, she noticed a couple of entries that stood out since they sounded so strange. One said "just because you're paranoid doesn't mean no one is following you" in bold type. Another said "are the three cases connected???" and it was followed by "If they call back, ask questions only they would know." The very last entry said, "so many hurting families with no one to help them." Did this have to do with the three missing children's cases? And who might call back? So many unanswered questions that she was afraid her head would explode.

To give herself a break, Rebecca turned to her sister's email and messages. So many people had sent condolences to her sister. It was odd to see a sympathy message in the inbox of a person who had passed, but fans of her YouTube channel obviously didn't have any other way to contact her but felt the need to reach out anyway. There were so many messages that Rebecca began to skim them before adding them to a new folder she created. She had been working on the project for about 15 minutes when she was stopped in her tracks by one. "This serves you right for ignoring me bitch! I told you something bad was going to happen to you if you kept it up. Rot in hell."

She swallowed deeply and stared at the message. It was signed "your biggest ex-fan" and came from an email address that began "exfan666." Rebecca wondered what had upset this person so badly. Was it someone her sister knew or was it just some random internet quack? And how could she find out? It was at times like this that she wished she had more technical knowledge. She created a new folder named "Questions" and moved the message into it. She would go through the rest of the messages and then return to any of them, like this one, that she wanted to look into further.

Once she had made her way through all the messages that had come in since her sister died, she started looking at the ones that were sent to her sister while she was still alive. There were notices of automatic withdrawal for utilities, notices for subscription renewals, and invoices for her business. One of the invoices was from a company called Spenser Network Pros with its tagline "Your Full-Service Technology Partner". Well, she mused if they were good enough for Natalie, they were good enough for her.

She picked up her phone and dialed the number on the invoice. After identifying herself, she set up an appointment for the next day at their office to speak with the person who had been working with Natalie on her technology.

After having a frozen meal for dinner, she opened a bottle of cabernet sauvignon and sat down on the couch in the living room. She sipped her wine and stared off into space. It had been a long day with a lot of ups and downs emotionally. She had been threatened, stared at, and whispered about. She had been dismissed by the local law enforcement and discovered someone who had hated her sister and wished her ill. As she thought about the day, her eyes wandered around the room, noticing all the personal touches her sister had included in her home. A deep sadness welled up within her and she took a deep, shuddering breath. She had been keeping herself busy by immersing herself in the documents, videos, and emails that made up Natalie's life and those activities had kept her grief in the background. But tonight, it was just her and her emotions. She leaned back and let the feelings roll over her, making no attempt to push them away. Her sister was worth every tear she shed.

Chapter Twenty-Five

Early the next morning, Rebecca pulled up in front of the Spenser Network Pros offices on Jorge Street. It was situated between a hair salon and an insurance agent in a strip mall that looked like thousands of other strip malls in America. She opened the front door and a bell above her tinkled like she had entered an old general store.

There was a reception desk near the front of the office that was covered in papers and white binders but there was no one sitting at it. A bright green head poked out of an office to her right.

"Rebecca? Come on in."

She entered the office and found herself in a world of chaos. There were books, binders, paper, and small electronic pieces on every flat space. She hesitated, unsure if she was supposed to enter the room further.

"Sorry, I meant to clear some space but the time got away from me," the green-haired man said as he grabbed a pile of papers from one of the chairs. "Have a seat."

She sat down and faced him, taking in his bright hair, combined with pale almost translucent skin, a pierced eyebrow, and a tattooed neck.

"Thank you for taking the time to meet with me," Rebecca began. "I won't take much of your time I don't think."

"No problem, first of all, I want to tell you how sorry I was to hear about Natalie,"

"Thank you, did you know her well.... um... I'm sorry I don't know your name" Rebecca said.

"Oh gosh, sorry, my name is Nate and I am the owner of Spencer Network Pros," he said. "I worked with Natalie on all of her technology from making sure she had enough bandwidth to ensuring her live streams worked properly, so I guess you could say I knew her pretty well," Nate explained.

Rebecca found it a bit jarring to listen to him talk because it was hard to reconcile his artsy almost alternative look with the owner of a company who talked about bandwidth and live streams. But he had kind eyes and now he was looking at her with sympathy.

"Do you think she was suicidal?" Rebecca asked the question before she had a chance to even think it through.

But his answer was as direct as her question. "No, I don't."

They sat looking at each other as though neither of them was quite sure what to do now that they had laid their thoughts out on the table.

"I've been going through her computer, looking at the videos she posted, the ones she was getting ready to post, checking out what she was researching, and trying to find evidence of this Peter guy" she finally said.

"Yeah, the Peter guy was news to me," Nate said. "She never once mentioned seeing anyone, she never acted depressed, and I was shocked when I heard what had happened."

"I wish I had found you a couple of days ago; it has been crazy feeling like I'm the only one who thinks her death was wrong on so many levels," Rebecca told him, relief evident in her voice and the way she seemed to slump further down into her chair.

"I wasn't sure if I should approach you," Nate explained. "I was afraid I would cause you pain if she had mentioned a boyfriend to you or if you happened to have known she was depressed. What do you think happened to her?"

"Honestly, I have no idea. All I know is there's no way the Natalie I knew for the last couple of years was depressed, she had no reason to keep a boyfriend secret...and a suicide pact? That's so not her!" she stated emphatically.

Rebecca was horrified to realize that tears had begun to stream down her cheeks. She hadn't realized how much she was beginning to question her own thoughts and emotions. The Sheriff was so adamant that she was wrong and that she was just refusing to face the reality of her sister's suicide. The townspeople looked at her as though she was an oddity and even her own husband thought she should just come home. These few words from Nate took the burden of doubt off her shoulders.

"Oh shit, I'm so sorry, I didn't mean to make you cry!" Nate exclaimed. "Here, take some tissues" he rummaged under a pile to the left of his desk and miraculously pulled out a box of facial tissue to hand her.

"No, it's okay, I'm just so happy to be able to talk to someone who isn't poo-pooing my doubts around my sister's death being a suicide" she wiped her nose and quickly pulled herself together.

Over the next hour or so they discussed Natalie, and what Rebecca had found on both Peter's and her sister's computers. She told him about every piece she had discovered that didn't align with her even having had a romance with Peter; the appointment Natalie said she had but didn't seem to have put in her calendar; the allegedly free days that were booked up on her calendar; her comments about "soulmates" and the talk about having a baby. She also told him about her unease over someone calling to cancel her electricity, the threatening letter delivered to her home, and the Sheriff's unwillingness to consider any of the concerns she brought to him.

As she was talking, in the back of her mind she realized she was putting a lot of faith in a stranger. She had just met Nate and she was sharing everything with him. What if he wasn't as trustworthy as he appeared? But she realized she couldn't keep going the way she had been. She needed someone to talk to and to bounce ideas off, if for no other reason than to keep her somewhat sane.

Once she had spilled everything to Nate, she felt exhausted, as though talking about it had taken what little strength she had left.

"Wow," Nate said, looking at her closely. "You've done a lot of work on this, haven't you?" She knew it was a rhetorical question, so she only smiled.

"So, what do I do now?" she asked.

"You mean what do we do now? I have been able to think of nothing else since I heard about Natalie and I want to help you get to the bottom of this."

She nodded, waiting for him to continue.

"I saw the video on her channel that she made with Peter, you said there are others?" "Yes, a couple. Some are just of Natalie and some of Peter."

"Okay, to start with, if I can take a look at them, I may be able to tell how legit they are," he said, taking out a piece of paper and searching for a pen. "The posted video is okay, but if I can examine the original files, that would be much better."

"I can do that," Rebecca said, pushing aside any anxiety she had about allowing anyone else to get ahold of what she now considered evidence. "I noticed there was a hate email in her inbox. I don't know if it is something to be looked into, but it was pretty vile."

"Forward that to me as well, I will see if I can figure out where it came from," Nate said, adding another item to the list he was writing. "I have access to the back end of her YouTube channel as I did some work for her there, but can I have your permission to go in again? I want to see if anything looks out of place."

"So, if you have a password to get in already then you don't need anything from me?" she asked.

"Correct, I'd just like your permission as I wouldn't go in on my own without notifying a client," he explained.

"Okay, go ahead." For some reason the idea that he had access to the technology made her feel almost vulnerable. As though he had been watching her while she was taping and loading the video she had made for her sister's channel. She knew it was silly, but it gave her a creepy feeling none the less.

"I'll send you a link where you can upload the videos. Once you upload them, I'll get to work on them," Nate said, setting his pen down. "That should be enough to get us started. Once I do that, it will either give us something to take to the Sheriff or not."

Rebecca stood up and reached over to shake his hand. His hand was warm, and he held hers gently as he looked into her eyes.

"I truly am sorry about Natalie, she was a lovely person with a very kind heart," Nate said. "The world is a little less without her."

Feeling her mood beginning to lift, Rebecca decided to grab a coffee at the shop just down from Nate's office. As she waited at the counter for her drink, she realized that it probably wasn't the best thing for her mental health to be cooped up in her sister's house all by herself, day in and day out. Although she still didn't like being stared at, at least she felt less isolated here. She sipped her coffee and thought about the things she needed to do once she did get back to the house and her sister's computer. She needed to send the videos and files to Nate and then she planned on looking at the comments on some of her sister's posted videos to see if the person who had sent the hate email had also commented there. While it probably was your run-of-the- mill hater, as had been suggested to her, it wouldn't hurt to look into it a little further. Hopefully, Nate would be able to work his technology magic. While Rebecca considered herself to be fairly knowledgeable about computers, it only took one conversation with an expert to realize she knew very little.

After her drink was finished, she walked out to her car and slipped in behind the wheel. As she pushed the start button, she frowned as she realized there was a split second of hesitancy before it caught. She made a mental note to herself to make an appointment for a checkup when she returned home.

She had to back up slightly as the car in front was parked too close for her to pull out easily. She smiled when she saw its license plates as it brought to mind memories of her and Natalie in the back seat of their parent's car, trying to beat each other in making sentences out of the license plate letters. It had been the start of a lifelong habit for Rebecca, and she had automatically converted the license plate of TCM 423 into 'too close to me'. She smiled and was grateful to have a warm memory of her sister that brought good feelings instead of pain.

Once she was on the road and driving, she noticed the steering was quite stiff and the car was not reacting as it usually did when she tried to turn. Suddenly, the car began to accelerate for no reason, and Rebecca panicked as she stepped on the brake and realized nothing was happening. Just then, a car pulled up beside her and she looked to see a man smiling over at her. She obviously wasn't thinking straight and she began to gesture as though somehow he would be able to realize she had lost control of her car and would do something to help. The man behind the wheel of the other car simply smiled at her and nodded before he sped up and passed her. She had barely registered the fact it was the car that had been parked in front of her before her car jumped the curb and headed straight towards the brick wall that ran the length of a park.

Chapter Twenty-Six

Her heart felt as though it was going to stop at that moment. Then, without giving herself a chance to think about it, she unbuckled her seatbelt, opened her door, and rolled out of the car.

All the air in her lungs was pushed out of her as she landed on the ground, and she hoped that somehow her body had listened to her and she had managed to tuck and roll.

As she lay on the ground, the only movement was her chest heaving as she gasped while trying to catch her breath. Suddenly she was surrounded by people, all talking at once.

"What on earth happened?"

"Are you hurt?"

"Why didn't you stop?"

"Is that Natalie's sister?"

Luckily, someone was helpful enough to call an ambulance as she wasn't sure where her phone was at that moment. She assumed it was in the car. The crowd was now arguing about whether she should move or not. One said if she felt okay to move, she should try to do so, while someone else said they had taken a first aid course and she shouldn't be relied on to know if she should move or not. She could have a broken back but be in shock and not able to feel the pain. There was no argument as far as she was concerned. She was staying put.

Once the ambulance arrived and she was in a cervical collar, she asked if they could retrieve her purse from the car. She wasn't sure what she was going to do with it, but she figured if she had her phone and her ID, she had options.

A couple of hours later, it was mid-afternoon, and she walked out of the emergency department's doors with a prescription for painkillers and an admonishment to take it easy for a few days. She had a visit from the Sheriff while she was in the emergency room and he took her statement about what had happened. As usual, he brushed her off and told her that her car had obviously malfunctioned. The car had been towed to a mechanics shop and she would probably hear from him in the next few days. But for Rebecca, who had seen the look on the face of the man who had driven beside her, there was no doubt that whatever had happened to her vehicle as she was driving was anything but an accident. However, she knew better than to try and convince the Sheriff of anything once he had made up his mind.

A nurse at the hospital had called a cab for her and as it pulled up in front of her sister's little white house, she had never been so happy to pay him and head up the front walkway. It seemed as though every muscle in her body was tightening up with each step she took. She poured herself a bath as hot as she could stand it and slowly sunk down into it until it was up to her chin. It was only then that she was able to begin processing what had happened. Someone had tried to kill her. She didn't care what the Sheriff thought, she knew what she had seen in the eyes of the man who had driven past her. She knew there was nothing wrong with her car this morning when she left to visit Nate. In the humid bathroom, submerged in near scalding water, she shivered.

SHE SPENT WHAT WAS left of the day curled up in the reading chair in her sister's conservatory. She used her tea to swallow the painkillers and stared out the unbroken part of the window. She supposed that at some point she would have to let Jason know what had happened. He would undoubtedly want her to drop everything and head home. And maybe she should.

Maybe she *was* in way over her head. She didn't know much more than when she had arrived, except that she knew her original feelings were correct. There was no way Natalie had taken her own life and now someone was trying to kill her. She fell asleep in that position as she pondered her options and when she awoke, the room was lit only by the outside streetlamp. As she moved to stand, her muscles protested and she groaned out loud but she also felt a steely resolve building up within her; there was no way whoever was responsible for her sister's death was going to get away with it. If they thought they were going to scare her off, they were sadly mistaken. If she had to die trying to find out what happened to her sister, then so be it.

With this thought in mind, she moved into the living room, turned on a light and sat at Natalie's computer once again. She had no time to spare so she might just as well get back into it.

SHE WOKE THE NEXT DAY to the sun streaming in through the curtains and a throbbing sensation at the base of her neck. The doctor at the emergency room had warned her that she would probably have increasing aches and pains for up to two weeks as her body reacted to the impact she had experienced. Getting dressed, she moved slowly and carefully so as not to jar anything further. She had poured a cup of coffee and was blowing across the top of it in an attempt to cool it when her phone rang.

"Yes?"

"Hi Rebecca, it's Nate."

"Hi Nate, did you find out anything new?"

"Sorry, no that isn't why I was calling. You didn't send the files until late last night so I'm just now getting to them," Nate explained.

"Oh, right sorry, my sense of time is a bit out of whack right now," she said.

"That's why I'm calling. I heard through the grapevine that you had an accident after you left my office? Are you okay?" Nate asked.

"I'm doing as well as can be expected. I have some sore muscles and a headache but nothing a good strong cup of coffee and a handful of painkillers can't handle."

"Was it a problem with your car?" Nate asked the question slowly and more quietly than he had been talking up to this point.

"You might say that it seemed to have a mind of its own and headed for a brick wall. The Sheriff thinks it's just a mechanical problem."

"A mind of its own, what do you mean?"

"The steering wheel jammed up and wouldn't respond when I tried to turn it, the car accelerated on its own and wouldn't brake no matter how hard I hit the pedal," Rebecca listed the ways her car had failed her.

"That many things going wrong all at once sounds more like a computer problem than something mechanical," Nate said. "As in, someone hacked your car's computer."

"I really was kinda hoping you would say that wasn't possible," Rebecca sighed.

"I wish I could, but unfortunately, it's absolutely possible," Nate said. "Best take care of yourself and maybe walk as much as you can until we find out what happened to Natalie."

REBECCA DECIDED TO take Nate's advice and stay in for the day. She was busy opening files on her sister's computer when she heard someone walk up her front steps. Tensing, she peeked through the living room curtains. It was Frank, the creepy window guy. She quickly jotted his name and the time down on her pad of paper. If she turned up dead at least she would have left a clue. She would still be dead, but they would know who did it.

She opened the front door and greeted him warily. Tipping his hat he told her he had the replacement window and asked if now was a good time for him to replace it? She told him to go ahead, and he smiled and turned around to collect his tools and the windowpane.

She knew she was probably being paranoid, but she just couldn't help it, especially after yesterday. She reached up and rubbed her neck. As he walked back towards the house, Rebecca picked up her cell phone and held it to her ear as though she was speaking to someone. As Frank entered the house, she told the person she was pretending she was talking with to hold on a second.

"Do you need anything from me?" she asked Frank.

"No, I'm good thanks."

"Thanks for holding, no, no it was the window guy coming to replace the glass in the conservatory," she told her imaginary friend. "Now what were you saying?" she walked towards the kitchen as though she talked to imaginary callers all the time.

After a few minutes, she hung up and went back to work at her sister's computer. She had found another file with random notes in it that Natalie had made regarding the cases she was researching. She seemed to be a big fan of typing out quick messages in order to keep her life in order. Of course, when you didn't know the file existed, it made it more difficult.

She was going through the file, confused by the order of notes. It took her a bit of scrolling up and down to realize her sister had added the most recent note to the top, not at the bottom end of the document. It made total sense once Rebecca figured it out.

At the top of the list it said "mtng w/SJM cntct Th. 29." Was she supposed to have a meeting regarding Sarah Jane Montgomery this Thursday, the 29th? What contact was she referring to? She looked the date up on her sister's calendar and there was nothing. No name and no time of any meeting. There were a couple more notes in the file and then "SJM cntct 5155557676". One of Iowa's area codes was 515 so she was certain this was a phone number.

Could this finally be a real lead? While she had been keeping an open mind and exploring all avenues, she had been feeling for a while that there was a connection between her sister's murder and the missing children. Her hands shaking slightly, she picked up her phone again and punched in the number. When a woman answered and said hello, Rebecca suddenly realized she hadn't considered what she was going to say.

"Hi, um, my name is Rebecca," she stammered. "You don't know me, but I came across your phone number in some papers of my sister's."

"Your sister?"

"Yes, my sister is Natalie Baker, I'm going through some of her stuff, and I came across your number in relation to Sarah Jane Montgomery."

The line went dead. Staring at her phone in disbelief, Rebecca briefly wondered if Nate had the ability to find out to who a phone number belonged. Then, her phone rang.

"Hello?"

"I'm sorry, I didn't mean to hang up on you like that, you just surprised me," the woman said.

"It's okay," Rebecca said. "But why was it such a shock?"

"I just didn't expect her to contact me until we were supposed to meet on thursday," she spoke as though she was being cautious about what she said.

"What were you meeting Natalie about?"

"Why are you calling me?" the woman ignored her question.

"I found your phone number among my sister's papers and I'm trying to figure out what she was working on," Rebecca hoped that her non-informative response would be enough to satisfy the woman. "But let's back up, what is your name?"

There was a pause at the other end as though the woman was considering whether to share that much information. Finally, she seemed to come to a conclusion and answered "Emily, my name is Emily."

Rebecca wasn't quite sure she believed her, but at least it was a place to start.

"Okay Emily," she began. "I know you had a meeting with my sister scheduled for this thursday but I'm not sure what it was about exactly. I know it was in relation to Sarah Jane Montgomery, but that is all I know."

"Why don't you just ask your sister?" the woman asked her.

Now it was Rebecca's turn to hesitate. It hadn't occurred to her that the woman didn't know Natalie had died. Of course, there was no reason for her to know but somehow Rebecca assumed that such a life-changing thing as Natalie no longer being in the world would of course be known by anyone who touched her world.

"My sister died," Rebecca said quietly. "I'm cleaning up her papers and stuff." "Died? How?" Emily demanded, shock in her voice.

"It's still being investigated," Rebecca said. Emily didn't need to know that she was talking to the only person investigating Natalie's death.

But Emily wasn't letting it go that easily. "Look, I just need to know if she died of natural causes," she pressed.

A tingle worked its way up Rebecca's spine. "No, it wasn't natural," she admitted.

"Oh shit, shit, shit," Emily cried out. "They must have got to her!" "Who got to her?" Rebecca asked.

Chapter Twenty-Seven

"I knew she shouldn't have been so public about what she was doing, I told her she needed to be careful," Emily continued.

"Who?" Rebecca cut her off. "Who are you talking about, who killed my sister?"

"Emily, who killed my sister?" Rebecca waited for Emily to finish hyperventilating on the other end of the phone. "I need to know what you know so I can find out what happened to Natalie."

"I don't think I can help you," Emily finally said. "I don't wanna die!"

Rebecca had to wait a few more seconds for Emily to compose herself again.

"Listen, if you can't help me in some way, at least give me something to point me in the right direction, please," She tried hard to keep the begging tone from her voice, but it came through loud and clear.

"Let me think about this and I'll get back to you," Emily told her. "But don't call me again, I'll contact you."

The line went dead. She stared at the phone in her hand in dismay. Just then, she looked up and saw Frank looking at her from the front door and her breath caught in her throat.

"Um, the window is in and it should be as good as new," he said. "Actually, in these old houses, it's probably better than new."

"Okay, thank you," she said. "How do you want me to pay?"

"I'll just email you an invoice and you can electronically transfer the money," Frank told her and with a tip of his hat, he was gone. It wasn't until later that she thought to wonder how he would know her email address.

After he left, she walked into the conservatory and looked at the new window. He was right, it was as good as new. Now she just needed to follow up with the Sheriff on the exterior of the house. She made a call to the police station, knowing she needed to get her mind off Emily and whether she was going to phone her back or not.

After speaking with the Sheriff and arranging for his nephew and a couple of his friends to paint the house the next day, she wandered around aimlessly. She tried to sit down at the computer and do more research but was unable to stay in one place long enough. Her mind was swirling in so many different directions, she couldn't land on any one thing for very long. Finally, she grabbed a notepad and pen and walked around, jotting things down as they came to her. She listed all the things she knew for sure. She knew that the only thing that tied her sister and Peter to each other were the videos. There was nothing else. No one had ever claimed to see them together, there were no phone calls from his number that came up on Natalie's phone, and her sister hadn't mentioned him once. While his mother had chatted with her online, she had never met Natalie face to face, even though they only lived an hour and a half away. While the videos were seen as evidence of suicide, her sister had given absolutely no indication of these intimate thoughts to the person who was closest to her.

Then there were the discrepancies between what was on those videos and what appeared to be going on in Natalie's life, such as her appointments, and her comments about wanting a child. Now someone had tried to hurt, if not outright kill her by hacking into her car's computer, her sister's house was vandalized and on top of this there was someone out there who knew something about the work Natalie was doing in the Sarah Jane Montgomery case. Why would Sheriff Briggs continue to brush her off? Had he even run the license plate number she gave him after her car accident? It was so frustrating to be in this alone, without any help from the Sheriff's office.

She finally placed the notepad on the table and went into the kitchen to open the refrigerator door. She stood there and looked into it for a few moments and then shut the door. After pacing some more, she decided she couldn't avoid talking to her husband any longer. First, she tried phoning him so they could have an actual conversation. When all she got was his voicemail, she fired off a text.

"Hey, can you give me a call when you have a minute?"

She made sure the volume was turned on and then threw the phone onto the kitchen counter. She began to go over in her mind what she knew about the Sarah Jane Montgomery case. She knew the child had gone missing from a daycare center and her parents were apparently in a violent relationship. The daycare owner and all their employees were cleared. Sarah Jane was never seen again. Then there was the baby who was stolen from a maternity ward and never seen again, where all the staff were cleared, but there were also allegations of domestic violence about the parents. Lastly, there was the second daycare abduction of baby Sabbie whose parents were part of a parolee discharge program. Was there somehow a connection between the less-than-savory parents and these childrens' abductions? At some point, she had picked up the paper and pen and began jotting notes down. Now, she sat staring at the list, tapping her pen against the paper. There were so many threads and she couldn't even determine if these, the last cases her sister was working on, were related to her death.

She jumped as her phone rang and she reached over to pick it up. It was Jason.

"Hi," she said cheerfully. She needed him in a good mood when she told him what happened to her in the car.

"Hi," his response was curt and sounded cold.

"What are you up to?" she asked.

"I'm working, when are you coming home?"

"I'm not sure yet, I have a lead on Nata..."

"You need to come home now," he interrupted before she could tell him what had happened since the last time they had spoken. "You've been gone long enough."

She was surprised to feel anger start to rise within her. This was an alien feeling when it came to Jason. Usually, she took what he said to heart and gave it due consideration. But today, after all she had been through and after so many people trying to tell her to stop what she was doing, she had had enough.

"I've been gone long enough for what, Jason?" she asked, ice in her voice.

Jason didn't seem to hear the tone of her voice, or he simply chose to just ignore it. "I want you to come home and be a wife. I've been patient up to now but enough is enough."

"What do you want me to do at home? What does being a wife mean to you Jason? Someone to make sure your dry cleaning is picked up and a meal is ready to re-heat?"

"Don't be ridiculous Becky, come home and we can get back to normal," he continued. "Normal? My sister died a horrible death, I think someone had her killed, and you just want me to come home and pretend everything is normal?" She was amazed she had never noticed before how emotionally tone-deaf he could be.

"We can talk about it when you get home," he had begun to take on a more cajoling tone, as though realizing that demanding she listen to him was not going to work like it usually would. "I miss you Becky and I miss my wife."

"I'm going to stay until it's time for me to come home Jason," she said firmly. There was silence at the other end of the line.

"I want you home by the end of the week Becky," Jason finally responded.

"Or what Jason? You'll take time off work and come get me?" Rebecca couldn't help making the jab about his workaholism.

"This isn't funny, be home by the end of the week," Jason hung up the phone.

She stood there, holding her cell phone in her hand, and thinking about the conversation she had just had with her husband, the man who was supposed to love her and be her number one supporter. She was facing the most difficult time she had ever experienced and not only was he not helping her, but he also didn't even care enough to know what was going on or to ask.

Chapter Twenty-Eight

The next morning, Rebecca was up early as she needed to make arrangements to have what was left of her car dealt with as it had been towed to the mechanic's shop. She had barely poured her orange juice when she heard a sharp rap at the front door. By the time she opened the door, no one was there, but an envelope had been left on her doorstep. She cautiously bent over to pick up the envelope, all the while looking around to see if she could see who had dropped it off. The trees near the edge of the property were moving, even though there was no wind, but she knew with her muscles still tense and aching from the car accident, she wouldn't have a chance of catching up to anyone. She sighed in frustration and went back into the house, envelope in hand.

The envelope was heavy and a bit bulky. When she opened it and cautiously looked inside, she saw a phone, the kind you buy in gas stations along with cards that provided minutes. She pulled it out and took a closer look. There was a post-it on top that said "I'll call you -E." She smiled as she realized that Emily had finally decided to talk to her, but on her own terms.

A half-hour later, the phone rang. She grabbed it and answered it quickly. She didn't want Emily to have second thoughts.

"Emily?"

"Hi, I'm sorry to be so dramatic, but I didn't want to take any chances," Emily explained. "I don't know what they know and what they don't know."

"It's okay, I'm fine with this," Rebecca reassured the anxious-sounding woman. "I'm just glad you decided to talk to me. Do you want to arrange to meet?"

"No!" The answer was swift and decisive. "I want to tell you what I know and then I want you to destroy the phone and forget you ever heard from me. I don't want to take any chance that either of us are being followed."

"You're scaring me Emily,"

"Haven't you figured it out yet Rebecca, you *should* be scared," Emily responded, sounding frustrated. "We are talking about some very unscrupulous people."

"Okay, why don't you start by telling me why you were supposed to meet with my sister?"

"I saw her video, on her YouTube station, the one where she was talking about Sarah Jane, the baby that was abducted so I reached out to her with some information," Emily began. "We were going to meet and talk about it. But they must have found out and had her killed."

"Who are *they*?" Rebecca asked, her voice thick with frustration.

"Just a minute, let me start at the beginning," Emily said impatiently. "Then you can ask me whatever you want, how about that?"

"Okay, I'm sorry, go ahead,"

"I saw the video and I contacted her because I had information about what happened the day Sarah Jane was abducted; I know what happened to her. I wanted to tell someone, someone who could warn others. You see, the worker that no one could ever find, Aleia? She was the one who helped abduct Sarah Jane. She had already handed the baby over to the abductors by the time she went in to use the washroom. The other worker had been asked to watch an empty stroller."

"But they checked her out, she stayed working for six months after Sarah Jane was abducted..." Rebecca began to question Emily but realized by the silence at the other end of the phone that she had promised to let Emily tell her what she knew. "Sorry, go ahead."

"Aleia had been approached almost a year before, well before Sarah Jane was even born. She was told that babies were being born to violent, drug-addicted parents who abused them and didn't deserve to be parents. She knew it was true because she had seen evidence of that in her job. She was working at another daycare when they approached her. She often felt upset and frustrated, knowing there was nothing she could do. She tried reporting one of the parents once and nothing had been done. Her employer had reprimanded her saying that unless it was obvious abuse, she shouldn't go to CPS. So, she watched neglected children go through daycare and there was nothing she could do. But these people who came to her, told her that they were on the children's side and that they would save these children, even if the government, CPS, and the courts wouldn't. They told her that there were so many couples who weren't able to have children who would do anything to raise them in a safe and happy home where they could be loved." Emily paused for a moment, taking a deep breath. Rebecca felt her heart sink as she realized where this was going.

"She believed them, she thought she was helping these children. She helped them abduct Sarah Jane. They told her the father had problems with his anger, that he beat his wife on a regular basis and that it was only a matter of time before he would begin to take it out on Sarah Jane, if he hadn't already done so. She was young, idealistic, and passionate about children. She wanted to protect them. So, she gave Sarah Jane to them. Then, she waited six months and after she was no longer under suspicion, she left town."

Rebecca waited patiently. She wanted more than anything to pepper Emily with questions about how she knew all of this, and where was Sarah Jane now? And who were "they"? But she knew if she spoke up, she might spook Emily and prevent her from finishing her story.

"After she moved away, they wanted her to do it again, this time with an even younger baby. Aleia wasn't sure about this one; she had met the parents and she didn't see anything that made her suspicious, even though they were telling her the baby's parents were horrible people. With Sarah Jane's parents, it was common knowledge that her father would hit her mother, but Aleia hadn't heard anything bad about this second family. And she was starting to become concerned, because the more questions she asked, the less she seemed to understand how they were helping these babies. When she asked them how they found the new parents and how they checked to make sure they would be good parents, they gave her evasive answers. When she wanted to know where Sarah Jane was, they told her it was for the babies own good that she not know. Sarah Jane was happily settling down with her new family and the less people who knew where she was, the better. And they began to really push her to take this other baby until finally she told them she just wasn't ready and that she didn't feel right about it. That is when things got bad for Aleia. They threatened to turn her in to the police and tell them what she had done with Sarah Jane. They said they would make it look like she had hurt Sarah Jane and that she was no longer alive. It was at this point that Aleia knew these people couldn't be who they had said they were. These were not vigilantes whose only concern was the children. They had shown their true side and Aleia was upset and horrified that she had helped them. She agonized over what had really happened to Sarah Jane and her role in her disappearance drove her almost to the brink. She only wanted to help children and now she feared she had delivered one into the hands of a group of evil people."

Emily was silent for a while and Rebecca struggled to take in all she had been told. Finally, she could no longer hold off with her questions.

"How are the Wakefield and Sabbie cases connected?"

"Natalie saw some similarities that convinced her they were related and that perhaps the babies were taken by the same group," Emily explained.

"Natalie was convinced there was a group who were taking babies from a bunch of different places?" Rebecca had no reason not to believe the possibility of an organized group that was abducting babies, but her mind still struggled to digest it.

"Yes, she had talked to enough people involved in both cases to make her believe they were all related somehow, even though Aleia was not involved in those other ones," Emily explained.

"So, what happened to Aleia? Did she take the baby like they wanted her to?"

"No, she didn't," Emily said quietly. "You don't need to know anything else except these are very, very dangerous people. Your sister got too close and I believe they killed her. I don't know the details around how she died and I don't need to. If it wasn't natural causes, then they killed her. Hell, even if it was from natural causes, I'm not sure I would be convinced it wasn't them."

"And you were going to meet my sister and tell her all of this?" Rebecca asked.

"Yes, and until I got your phone call, I had every intention of following through with that. But I'm not going to die over this. I have shared with you what I know, the rest is up to you, I'm not saying another word to anyone about it."

"But without you to substantiate this, I can't take it to law enforcement or anything," Rebecca began to protest.

"I don't care, I have done what I can do and as it is I am sticking my neck out. I could have kept quiet and protected myself, but this is it."

"Just one more question, please?"

"What?"

"Did Peter have anything to do with this?" Rebecca asked, trying to piece together all the parts of the puzzle.

"Peter who?"

"Supposedly he was my sister's soulmate, he died with her," Rebecca said.

"I don't know anything about that, she didn't mention anyone by that name," Emily responded. "I have to go now, please turn your phone off, pound it with a rock or flush it down the toilet or something. Anything to get rid of it. I'm going to do the same with my phone, there can be nothing to show we spoke or I am dead."

Chapter Twenty-Nine

With the rest of the day stretching out in front of her, Rebecca was at a loss as to where to go from here. She had way more information than she had before, but no proof of anything.

Maybe a walk would help get the blood pumping through her aching muscles and clear her head a bit. There was something about someone trying to kill you that makes a person a bit paranoid and she knew she would be looking over her shoulder the whole time but she couldn't stay here forever. It had felt so good to get out and sit in the coffee shop yesterday that she knew she needed more of it. Spending days at a time in the home where her sister died, poring through her files, old videos and documents was not good for her.

She slipped into her shoes, grabbed the keys and her wallet, and headed out. The boys the Sheriff had lined up would be coming around soon to get started on painting the house and she wanted to be back in time to greet them. Apparently, they were going to go and pick up the paint and some brushes so they would be ready to get started as soon as they arrived. She couldn't wait to get the red paint with its awful words and all it signified off the house.

She wasn't sure how much she believed and how much she trusted what Emily had told her, but it all fit. There was an organized group of people who were getting people to steal babies under the pretense of protecting them. But there was now some question as to whether those babies were actually saved from anything or even who they may have been handed over to. Her sister began researching Sarah Jane

Montgomery's cold case and putting some of the pieces together. She posted videos on her channel and resurrected the case. She was too close and so they killed her.

So far, while it seemed pretty far-fetched, it made a twisted kind of sense. But then she came up against her sister's death and the presence of Peter. The only link to them was the videos, but even if she pretended the videos didn't exist, it didn't make any sense. If Peter was involved with this group and was tasked with shutting her sister up, why kill himself? Was there a third person there the night she was killed? Did they kill both Peter and Natalie? That might work except why would Natalie let them into her home in the first place? Was it someone she knew and trusted? And all these questions were if she ignored the presence of the videos. Which she couldn't. Their existence muddied the water even more. Why had her sister never mentioned Peter? Why would her sister have been involved in making those videos if she wasn't depressed? If she was depressed, why did Rebecca not know?

Her head began to ache with all the unanswered questions. As she strolled along the quiet streets, she took a deep breath and tried to think about something else, even for a few moments. She used techniques she had learned during a mindfulness class she had taken. She focused on the leaves, the trees, and what was real and solid right now, in this very minute. She paid attention to the breeze on her arms as she swung them by her side. The feeling of the muscles in her legs and hips as they lifted her legs and propelled her forward. By clearing her mind, she left room for other thoughts. Like Jason. She groaned as his face flashed before her eyes. What was she going to do about her marriage? While she had always known her relationship with Jason wasn't exactly fireworks and roses, her sister's death had made it very apparent that her husband cared little for what was important to her.

So much had changed since her sister died, not least her outlook on life. Before, she thought Jason was all she needed and that she wouldn't be able to live without him. Now she saw clearly that she could live without him; without waiting around at home for him to finish work or for her to get a call to work as a substitute for the day. She felt as though she had been walking around in a daze for the last few years and was just now seeing things clearly. Why had it been enough for her for so long? That was a question for the therapist she was sure she would be having on speed dial by the time all of this was over.

Rounding the corner at the end of her sister's street, she saw a pickup truck pulled in front of the house and a handful of young guys milling around. She picked up her speed and quickly shoulder-checked before crossing the street to the right side. She was halfway across the road, her eyes on the pickup when she heard a vehicle behind her. She knew instinctively it was too close and was going too fast, so she immediately dove toward the sidewalk. She could have sworn she felt the vehicle swipe her pant leg and for the second time in as many days, she rolled out of the way. A blur of black careened down the street, not even stopping to see if she was okay. Her heart was pounding so loudly that her head hurt from the blood pounding into it. She could vaguely hear footsteps running down the sidewalk towards her as she pulled herself into a sitting position. A bunch of teenagers circled her, their faces looking shocked.

"Are you okay?" one of them asked.

"I think so, someone wanna give me a hand?" she reached up and one of the boys grabbed her hand and helped her to her feet.

"You sure you should be moving, should we call the ambulance?" Another asked.

"Ha! No, this is nothing compared to yesterday,"

The boys looked at her, confusion evident on their faces.

"Never mind, it's an inside joke," she said as she began to walk the rest of the way toward Natalie's house.

"That guy was trying to hit you, I think we should call the Sheriff," one of the boys spoke up. The others murmured their agreement.

"No, no there's no point," Rebecca waved them off. The Sheriff had been less than useful and she didn't think one measly attempted hit-and-run was going to change anything.

"I really think we should," another boy said. "The Sheriff is my uncle, and he needs to know someone is going around town trying to run people over." He was already pulling out his cell phone and Rebecca didn't have the heart to try and explain to him that his uncle wasn't going to help her.

"Did anyone catch the license plates?" the same boy asked.

"I only saw the first two letters before it was gone; it was going like a bat out of hell!" his friend answered, his voice sounding awed. "It was TC."

"Well, that isn't very helpful," the Sheriff's nephew said.

"The plates were TCM 423" Rebecca told them. The group turned to look at her, shock on their faces. How had she managed to see them when she was the one sprawled out on the sidewalk? "Never mind," she waved them off and entered the front door of the house. "Let me know if you need a drink or to use the washroom. Oh, and thanks for agreeing to paint the house."

As she closed the door behind her, she heard the Sheriff's nephew say "Uncle Art? I think you should know something..."

Chapter Thirty

Sheriff Briggs found Rebecca sitting at her kitchen table with a glass of wine in one hand and her cell phone in the other.

"The door was open, I called out," he said hesitantly.

"Yah, all good, come on in," Rebecca responded with little to no inflection in her voice.

"My nephew Rob said someone tried to run you down?" Sheriff Briggs asked her. "Yup, right out there, in broad daylight."

His eyebrows came together as he looked at her carefully. "Are you okay?"

"Of course, I am. I'm hunky dory!" she raised her glass to him and took a sip out of her wineglass as she spoke.

"Rob said you didn't think he should call me, why is that?"

"Shouldn't the question be why? My non-depressed sister supposedly took her own life with a boyfriend she didn't have and you aren't interested, "she laughed cynically. "Someone tries to kill me by hacking into my car and you shrug, so what's a hit and run?"

He looked at her and shook his head and she could have sworn she saw him roll his eyes. "Knock it off Robertson, I'm here, ain't I?"

"Oh, thank you sir, thank you so much for taking time out of your day!"

He raised one eyebrow and pursed his lips while pulling out his notepad. "Did you get a look at the driver of the car?"

"Nope, not even a glimpse."

"But you saw the license plate?"

"Nope, not even a glimpse."

He lowered his notepad in frustration. "Rob said you knew the license plate of the car. Was he right, did you see it?"

"He's right, I know the plate number and no, I did not see it," she told him.

He waited for her to go on, refusing to engage in her game any longer. Rebecca took another drink of wine and continued to stare at him challengingly. Their game of chicken was eventually broken by Briggs.

"Come on, I don't have all day, can we just do this? What is the license number?"

"You already have it, Sheriff. It's the same as the car that passed me when my car was hacked. It was the same person," she stated.

"How do you know that?" he asked.

"It was a black car, it tried to hit me, and your nephew said the first two digits of the license were TC. The license plate on the other car was TCM 432," she explained slowly, as though talking to a child. "So, if you add two and two, you get four."

"So, if I have this right, you didn't see the license plate of the car that tried to run you down today, but because a bystander saw the first two parts of the license plate and they are the same as the car you claim hacked your car, you're drawing the conclusion that it was the same car?"

Rebecca stared at him, shaking her head slightly. The conversation was happening just the way she expected. It was a waste of time to even talk to him. "I have some work to do, is there anything else you need?" she asked.

"I'll run the plates and let you know if anything comes up," Sheriff Briggs said as he put his notepad away.

Rebecca couldn't help the guffaw that came out of her at that moment. When Briggs looked at her, his eyebrows coming together sharply, she offered an explanation.

"You're going to run the plates the same way you did when I gave you the information the first time?" she mocked him. Part of her was watching their exchange with surprise as she wasn't usually so forward and aggressive with her contempt. But she was fed up and wasn't prepared to be patronized by this man any longer. "You had those plate numbers yesterday and have had plenty of time to find out who they belong to."

"I can see we're not able to have a constructive conversation about this, so I'll see myself out," Sheriff Briggs said as he turned around and left.

"Hey Sheriff!" Rebecca called out and he turned around. "Your nephew seems like a good kid."

STIRRING A JUG OF JUICE, Rebecca stared out into the backyard. She could hear the boys laughing as they moved ladders and pails around outside. She had made a pile of sandwiches to take to them as well. They had been working hard all morning and she was pleased to see that they would probably be done today. Her heartrate had finally returned to normal and with it, her mood had improved. She probably shouldn't have taken it out on the Sheriff, but she had felt so helpless when it really sank in that someone had tried to kill her twice in as many days. She didn't expect any help from Briggs, but at least he said he would run the plates. At this point, it was a waiting game as she waited for him to do his job and for Nate to work his magic on the files she had sent him.

When she put the plate of sandwiches and the jug of juice down on the picnic table in the backyard, she thought she was going to get trampled by a group of marauding teenagers so she went back inside to see what more she could find to feed them. As she entered the house, she heard her cell phone ringing. It was sitting on the kitchen table, and she hurried to catch it before whoever was calling her hung up.

"Hi Becky," Jason said.

"Hi Jason," Rebecca was surprised to hear his voice as he so rarely called. His preferred mode of communication tended to be texting.

"I'm concerned about you, and I wanted to check in and see if everything is okay," he spoke quietly.

"I'm fine, how are you?" She saw no reason to tell him about the latest incident with the black car. He would just use it to try and force her to come home and Rebecca knew she wasn't going anywhere. To bring it up would just invite another fight.

"Honestly? I'm not doing so good," he responded. "I miss my wife and I want her home."

"I know you do, and I'm sorry I'm not there, but I have to finish what I have started here," she answered, keeping her voice calm. He was talking rationally, and she wanted to keep it that way.

"Are you wanting to finish what you started or what Natalie started?" he asked.

Rebecca sat quietly; while the question could be viewed as trying to start a fight, she elected to take it at face value.

"I guess it's both." She didn't elaborate because she wasn't sure if she could explain to her husband that somehow what her sister had been involved in had become something very personal and important to her too.

"What does that even mean Becky?" He sounded frustrated, as though the agitation he had been holding at bay was seeping through.

"It means this is important to me and I'm asking you to respect that," Rebecca finally said.

"No, that isn't what you're asking me to do, *Becky*. What you're asking me to do is put up with your sister coming first yet again, even when she's dead!" By the end of the sentence, he was almost yelling at her.

Stunned, she stood with her mouth agape. Where on earth had this come from?

"What do you mean, Jason?" she asked as she worked to keep her voice neutral and quiet.

"I mean exactly what I said. You've always put your sister before me, you did it when she was alive and you're doing it still." The words gushed out of Jason as though once he started, he was unable to control what he was saying. "Natalie this and Natalie that, no one is as perfect as my sister Natalie."

She couldn't believe what she was hearing. Rebecca knew her sister didn't like Jason, but he had never let on that he felt this way about her as well. Sure, he hadn't been as upset by her death as she was, but that was to be expected; after all it was her sister. But to hold a grudge against a dead person? To be jealous of them?

"I, I can't believe you're saying this," she managed to stutter.

"Why? Why is it so shocking that I'm upset about a woman who has hated me since the day she met me? A woman who made it clear she thought I wasn't good enough for you." He sounded like he was getting more and more wound up so Rebecca kept quiet, she didn't want to encourage him to say any more.

He sounded as though he was panting on the other end of the phone. "She was a bitch to me, and you were fine with it," he went on. "And now, even in death she is influencing you and now she's causing people to try and kill you, am I not supposed to have feelings about that?"

"I don't think this conversation is going anywhere constructive," Rebecca answered. "Why don't we hang up before we both say something we will really regret."

"Fine, but don't bother talking to me until you're willing to come home and forget this whole thing," Jason's end of the phone went silent. Setting her phone down slowly, she took a deep breath and grabbed the fruit bowl off the table to take to the ravenous teenagers working on her house.

It wasn't until she was outside again when it suddenly struck her that Jason knew someone was trying to kill her. She hadn't told him about the problems with her car.

Chapter Thirty-One

By the end of the day, her house was freshly painted, and the boys were sent on their way. She jotted down Rob's email address so she could pay him and he could then divvy it up with his friends. She had been honest with the Sheriff when she said Rob was a good kid and both he and his friends had been polite and respectful all day. The house looked so much better, and tears came to her eyes as she stood on the front sidewalk and looked at it. Her sister would have been so pleased as Rebecca knew she was keen to get the house painted.

She went back into the house and sat down to eat the pizza she had ordered. As she ate, she scrolled through her sister's Facebook feed. There were so many people posting messages of condolences and questions. There was no way she could ever get through all of them and answer the questions. She switched over to Instagram where there was an equal number of posts. Overwhelmed, she threw the phone on the table. She was shocked when a phone rang until she realized it was hers, not her sister's. Laughing at herself, she stood up and went over to the counter to answer it.

"Hi Rebecca?" It was Nate. "Yes, hi."

"I'm done going through the stuff you sent me from your sister," Nate said, sounding a bit breathless.

"Oh great, did you figure anything out?" Rebecca asked.

"Yes, I certainly did," Nate said. "We need to talk about what we found, I think I figured out how and why your sister was killed."

Her heart beat loudly in her chest and she grabbed at the table for support. "You did? How? Why? What do you know?" the words tumbled out of her too fast for Nate to answer.

"We need to talk in person, I want to show you some things on the videos and explain them to you."

"Okay, I don't have a vehicle yet, but maybe I can call a cab," she said, looking around the room as though the answer to her transportation problems was lying around in plain sight.

"No, no, I can come to you, I'll just bring my laptop," Nate said. "Give me half an hour to get some stuff together and I'll head over to your place, can you text me your address?"

"I'll do that."

After they hung up, and she sent her address to him, Rebecca began to pace. Every nerve in her body felt like it was supercharged and jumping. She tried to sit down, but within a minute she was standing again, tapping her hands against her leg. What had Nate discovered? And how could the documents and videos he sent have told him everything? She had been over them so many times. She hoped he had some proof of whatever he discovered and that it wasn't just speculation. She needed something she could take to the Sheriff. She looked at the clock on her phone and groaned when she realized only four minutes had gone by. She couldn't recall a time when she felt more helpless. Or a time when she wished she had a vehicle at the very least.

Although to be honest, she wasn't sure she would be able to get in a car and drive again, at least not without a whole lot of anxiety. And who was she kidding, even walking ran the risk of becoming traumatic. Whoever was behind this had really messed with her transportation options.

Rather than watch the minutes tick slowly by, she poured herself some juice and grabbed a bunch of cookbooks that were tucked away in the kitchen cupboard above the stove. She might as well start going through these as she was going to have to make some decisions about

Natalie's stuff sooner or later. Her sister loved cookbooks. She wasn't much into cooking, but cookbooks and cooking tv shows were her favorite. Rebecca smiled about her sister's culinary quirkiness. She had been teased mercilessly about it by every boyfriend she ever had and by Rebecca herself. She had cookbooks on French cooking, how to make pasta and one called *50 Different Bread Recipes for the Busy Career Woman*. She noticed a piece of paper sticking out of one of the books and she flipped to that page and unfolded the piece of paper. It was a shopping list and along the side of the list was a note that said: "call Reb. wish happy b.day." Tears welled up in her eyes and she felt the loss of her sister keenly.

AFTER SHE HAD WIPED her tears and blown her nose, Rebecca put the cookbooks back where she had found them and reached for her phone. It was now twenty-five minutes since she had spoken with Nate. He should be coming by at any time. She went to the bathroom and splashed some cool water on her face and then ran some lipstick over her lips. Then she sat on the chair in the living room, occasionally glancing out the window anxiously when she heard a noise. By 8:45 pm she began to pace the house again, always coming back to look out the front window.

Where was Nate? She didn't know him well enough to know if he was one of these chronically late people but he sounded pretty excited when he called her, so surely he didn't get busy with something else and forget. She checked her phone to see if she had missed a call or a text from him. Nothing. What had happened to him?

"Hey, Nate, sorry to bug but are you coming over?" she texted him. Maybe he was driving and couldn't look at his texts, which would mean that his not answering was a good sign. She waited ten more minutes, reasoning that if he had been driving, he should have arrived by now.

Then, she phoned him, but no one answered. It was nine now and she wasn't sure what she should do.

She had no transportation, and he wasn't answering his phone or texts. So, there was nothing she could do but wait. She almost smiled when she imagined calling the Sheriff to report Nate missing because he was half an hour late. She went over to her sister's computer and sat down, wondering if she should send him an email. Why not? If he thought she was acting stalkerish, it was his own fault for being late and leaving her hanging.

For the next hour, Rebecca alternated between checking her phone for a text and her inbox for an email. She tested her phone to make sure it was still able to make calls and that nothing was wrong with it. It was fine. What the hell was going on? By this time it was almost eleven, and she knew that nothing was going to happen tonight. He wasn't coming around over two hours later than they had scheduled and she had exhausted all avenues for trying to contact him. She rummaged through her sister's medicine cabinet for some sleeping pills her sister told her once that she kept on hand for her bouts of insomnia. She took a pill, washed it down with water, and crawled into bed.

Damn Nate for putting her through this. He had better hope he had at least broken a bone, or she was going to give him one when she found him tomorrow.

Chapter Thirty-Two

The minute her eyes opened in the morning, she reached for her phone. Nothing from Nate, but there was a text from Sheriff Briggs asking her to contact him when she woke. She checked the time and it was only 7:30. Briggs had sent the text at 6:45. Her heart began to pound faster and she remembered what she had thought about Nate and broken bones the night before. As she dialed the Sheriff, she muttered to herself that she hadn't meant anything by it and no, of course she didn't hope he had been hurt. Please, don't be hurt, Nate.

"Sheriff Briggs," a gruff familiar voice said.

"It's Rebecca, you asked me to contact you when I got up?" she said in a voice still slightly husky from sleep. "Is everything okay?"

"I'm not really sure to be honest," for the first time since she met him, Briggs sounded uncertain. "I ran those plates and it seems to have poked a bear."

Rebecca's wasn't sure what to think. She had been steeling herself against news about Nate and an accident that she found it hard to digest what he was saying.

"You mean this isn't about Nate?"

"Nate? Nate who?" Briggs asked.

"Nate the computer guy," she explained.

"Why would I be calling you about Nate the computer guy?"

"I don't know, I've been trying to get a hold of him and I can't. I was afraid something had happened to him."

There was silence at the other end of the line as the Sheriff seemed to take in what she was saying. "I don't know anything about Nate or even how you know him so I wouldn't be calling you about him, but we can discuss Nate later."

"Okay, why did you call then?" Rebecca felt as though she had just exited a bad game of who's on first.

"As I was saying, I ran those plates you gave me. Registered to someone I don't recognize as being local. I was gonna leave it at that but then I received a call from the Federal Bureau of Investigation."

"The FBI?" she interrupted.

"Yes, the FBI, they wanted to know why I was running that those plates. They wanted to tell me not to take the owner in on anything."

"Why would they do that?" she asked.

"Well gee, why didn't I think to ask them that?" Briggs said sarcastically. "I did ask them. They said it had to do with an ongoing investigation and they wanted to talk."

There was silence for a split second before Rebecca asked why he was calling to tell her this information. "While I appreciate being kept in the loop, it isn't exactly, um, something I'm used to from you."

"It wasn't my idea, believe me, but I told the FBI why I was running the plates and they want to meet us. You and me. They want to talk."

CONFLICTED WOULD BE a mild word to describe how Rebecca felt as she prepared for the arrival of Sheriff Briggs and the FBI. She was still very worried about Nate's whereabouts, but she was also happy to have the FBI brought into the case. She wasn't sure what their sudden interest meant, but she reasoned that it couldn't possibly be a bad thing. Sheriff Briggs had been less than helpful to this point and maybe bringing in people who were supposed to know what they were doing would help things move along. But what about the information Nate had found? All these thoughts were swirling through her mind when she heard a vehicle pull up to the house. She froze as she usually couldn't hear when someone came to see her, but this car was very loud.

Looking out the window, she saw a beat-up extended cab Ford pickup with its muffler dangling, looking as though any minute it would fall to the ground.

Her eyes squinted as she watched three men exit from the truck, the driver was a tall, lean, bald man with tattoos up and down his forearms and wearing a pair of jeans that were full of rips and tears, and a Carhartt jacket. The other man was of similar height but had light, almost white hair, and a ruddy complexion. When Rebecca caught sight of the third man as he tried to heave himself out of the back seat of the truth and stand up with some semblance of dignity beside the other men, she had to clasp her hand over her mouth to stifle a giggle. Sheriff Briggs looked comically out of place next to what she assumed now were his FBI counterparts, although she had no idea why they were dressed that way.

She opened the door before they had a chance to knock and came face to face with the bald man who had driven the truck.

"Ms. Robertson?" he asked in a deep voice.

"Yes, come on in," she stepped aside so he could enter, followed by who she assumed was his colleague and Sheriff Briggs brought up the rear.

"I assume you are the FBI?" she got right to the point.

"Yes, would you like to see some ID?" the blonde asked, reaching into his pocket. "We're on the job and it requires we dress pretty casual, so I apologize if we alarmed you at all."

She thought that was one way to subtly say you are working undercover without telling someone you are working undercover. She checked his ID which told her his name was Special Agent Nick Reinhold. She handed it back to him and then turned to take the other agent's ID which identified him as Special Agent Ian Rudder.

"Well, Special Agents Reinhold and Rudder, Sheriff Briggs says you are interested in talking to me about the car that has been trying to kill me?"

"Yes, the license plate number was flagged and when Sheriff Briggs ran it, we wanted to know why," Rudder said.

"Why is this car and this person so important to you?" she asked.

The two men looked at each other, as though communicating silently. Rebecca looked from one of the men to the other.

"Would it help if I showed you mine first?" she tilted her head to the side and raised her eyebrows.

Sheriff Brigg's head swiveled around to glare at her, and she had the distinct impression he wanted to impress these two agents and he was more than a little concerned that she was going to embarrass him in front of them.

"That might be helpful," Rudder agreed. She gestured for the men to take a seat at the kitchen table and she sat down herself. She considered offering them a drink, but she wasn't feeling up to the niceties of hosting at the moment.

"Well, my sister is, or rather was a true crime youtuber who was investigating a child abduction ring when she got too close to the truth. Somehow, they had her killed and staged it to look like a double suicide. I have been trying to get to the bottom of it and now they are trying to kill me."

She watched the men to gauge their reaction to what she had said. Briggs could catch flies as his mouth was hanging so far open. Of course, this was the first time he was hearing about the child abduction stuff. But what interested her was the reaction of the two special agents. They made a couple of scribbles on the notepads they had pulled out. Neither of them seemed shocked by what she had disclosed. She was relieved that they seemed to be taking what she was saying seriously, but on the other hand, it struck a shaft of fear into her as she acknowledged that it meant she was involved in something very, very serious.

"Tells us more about the abduction ring, what did you learn and how?" One of the agents prompted her to continue.

"I spoke with someone who somehow knew the person who abducted Sarah Jane Montgomery. That was the first case my sister was looking into. She interviewed people about it and someone contacted her with information. Somehow, she pieced it together with a couple of other cases. I don't know how much my sister knew when she died but she was obviously making someone very uneasy." She waited to let them take in what she was saying, but only Briggs seemed at all overwhelmed or disbelieving.

"Now Rebecca, don't get started on your sister. We have irrefutable proof that she killed herself, and the same with Peter." As he talked, Briggs looked at her as though she was a foolish child who needed to be told things over and over.

"Can we have the name and contact information of the person who told you about the ring?" Agent Rudder ignored Brigg's comment.

"I'm afraid not, I only know her name was Emily, while I have a phone number that I originally contacted her on, she seems to have gone underground and we only talked on burner phones. I don't think she will want to talk to anyone about it, she made that pretty clear."

There was a thick silence as the agents finished making more notes. Briggs moved around in his seat, unsure what to add to the conversation but feeling the situation slip out of his control.

Finally, Rebecca broke the quiet: "So, are you going to show me yours now?"

Special Agent Rudder closed his notepad and leaned back in his chair. He stared at her with a speculative gleam that made her uncomfortable.

"The car is registered to Darrell Brantley. He works for an organization that's into human trafficking, drugs, prostitution and you name it. If there is a way to make some money, they have at least dabbled in it. Including selling babies."

"And that is the man who tried to kill me?"

"We don't know for sure if he was driving the car that tried to hit you as apparently you didn't get a glimpse of the driver, but if it wasn't him, it was someone that is tied to him and the organization."

"So, if you know all of this, why are these people still roaming the streets?" She asked.

"We don't have the proof we need; they are good at what they do and they run a tight ship. There are few people who are privy to the kind of information we need."

She looked back and forth between the two agents as she processed what she had heard. "And you don't want us to pursue the attempted hit and run because you want to keep trying to get the proof you need?" Rebecca guessed.

There was silence as the two men stared at her in silence. She looked over at Briggs and he looked as clueless as she felt. It made sense that they didn't want her rocking the boat, but why weren't they agreeing with her? Why were they just sitting there looking at her with an odd intensity?

"What?" she finally blurted out.

"Ms. Robertson, you have managed to do something we haven't been able to do; you've managed to get them in a reactive state, and they have gotten sloppy. Usually, they take care of people who get in their way swiftly and in a way that is final."

"Like my sister?"

"We don't know about that, it looks suspicious, but we really can't be certain yet," Reinhold answered. "While I'm not big on coincidences, the fact is that she could have been getting too close to the truth and she could have taken her own life. The two things can both be true. Sheriff Briggs said there are videos and written notes left by your sister and the man she died with?" He looked towards the Sheriff to see him nodding in confirmation.

"But" Rudder interjected. "If we are able to put this group behind bars, we may learn more about your sister if, in fact, they were responsible for her death."

"That's right," Reinhold nodded. "Which brings us to why we wanted to talk to you."

Now it was time for Rebecca to sit in silence, waiting for them to continue. They obviously had come here with an agenda, and she wanted to know what that was.

"We have been working to draw out the top guy in this organization, but we haven't been able to as yet," Reinhold began. "His right-hand man, Darrell Brantley, usually does the dirty work. Brantley is patient and meticulous and he doesn't jump in or do things without thinking it through. He plans what he is going to do and makes sure he covers his tracks. But the top guy, Alexander Mordaugh, he's a different story. When he gets involved, things tend to get messy. He reacts and flies off the handle and does things like ordering a hit-and-run in a 'company' car. Everything is pointing to Mordaugh being directly involved in this and if that is true, we have a unique opportunity to get directly to him," Reinhold stated. "What we want is for you to lead us to him. We want you to let him get you."

Rebecca continued to stare at him. She wasn't sure what she had expected him to say, but that certainly wasn't it.

"Why? and how?"

"We want you to go on your sister's YouTube channel and state that you have found some evidence you're planning to take to the authorities, and it is going to blow the lid right off the Sarah Jane Montgomery case. You can explain that this evidence is in a safe place right now but you are excited to wrap up the last case your sister was working on. Hopefully, that will cause them to come for you, but this time they will want you alive so they can get their hands on the evidence."

"You seem to have given this a lot of thought," Rebecca frowned slightly as she realized they knew more about what her sister had been doing than they were letting on.

"We've both been working on this case for a couple of years now, we are ready to wrap it up and move on. We want this creep put away for a long, long time and we want you to help us," Rudder said.

Her mind was racing a mile a minute as she processed what they were asking from her. She had wanted the authorities to take things seriously and believe what she was telling them and now it was happening. But they were asking her to put herself out there as bait for an organized crime ring that wouldn't hesitate to torture and kill her, of that she was sure. But what option did she have? She had come to the end of what she could do herself.

"I will do it, but on one condition," she told them. "Nate from Spenser Network Pros was working on the videos and documents I sent him that my sister apparently created. He said he had discovered something, but I haven't been able to get a hold of him. If I help you with this, will you give Nate whatever help you can provide whether it is equipment, knowledge, or manpower?"

"We can do that, but you say you can't find him now?" Rudder asked. "When did you hear from him last and what did he say?"

"He said he had figured out something about my sister's death and that he wanted to show me something; he was supposed to come over but he never did. He isn't answering texts, phone calls, or emails. I've been concerned but I don't even have access to transportation now, thanks to this group."

"Sheriff Briggs, will you be able to swing by his place and check on things? I assume you know where you can find him?" Rudder turned to ask Briggs. Conflicting emotions crossed the Sheriff's face. On one hand, he looked pleased to be brought into things, but on the other hand, he wasn't happy to be told what to do in his own jurisdiction. But finally, he agreed.

"We'll be back in touch within a few hours," Rudder explained to Rebecca. "We need to make arrangements to protect you by installing things like tracking devices, and microphones. We will also need to call in enough agents to watch you around the clock."

"Okay, I'll wait to hear from you," Rebecca nodded, her mouth had become dry as what she had agreed to do began to sink in.

Chapter Thirty-Three

The hours crawled by as Rebecca waited to hear back from the FBI. It was impossible to do anything but pace and run the possibilities through her head. Was this what would lead to some answers about her sister's death? Would it be her sister's legacy to help bring down an organized crime syndicate? Was she being foolish to become involved in this at all? She knew if she asked Jason, he would tell her she was not only being foolish but delusional. She didn't understand why he seemed to be so deliberately obtuse as to why this was important to her. How many years had he known her? How many years had he witnessed the deep relationship between she and her sister? Yes, what she was about to do was dangerous and maybe even foolhardy, but she had no choice.

About two hours after the men had left, her cell phone rang. It was Briggs. He sounded breathless and as though he was speaking into a long tube.

"It's the Sheriff," he identified himself.

"Yes, I know, what's up? Did you talk to Nate?"

"No, I'm afraid not, I..." the rest of what he said sounded garbled and Rebecca had to strain to listen.

"What was that?"

"I said, I wasn't able to talk to Nate but unfortunately, we did find him," Briggs said. This time the last few words sounded as though they were shouted because just then the reception seemed to improve.

"What? What happened? And where are you?"

"I'm out at Hawkeye Point, we found Nate but unfortunately he is dead," Sheriff Briggs told her. He sounded overwhelmed and upset.

"What? Oh shit, no!" Rebecca flopped down on the couch and rested her head in her hand while keeping the phone to her ear. "They got to him!"

"We're still not certain what happened bu..." the line crackled again and cut in and out for about 20 seconds before clearing up.

> "You cut out again, what did you say?" Rebecca said, frustration beginning to lace her voice. "The reception out here is crap, I'll call you when I get back to town, but it might be a while, our friends here say to tell you it might not be until tomorrow morning before they can get things set up for you," Briggs explained. "They're looking things over here first."

"I understand, but Briggs... what happened to him?" she asked but she wasn't totally sure she wanted to know the details.

"We found his car in a steep ditch, and he seems to have hit his head on the windshield as it's shattered. Beyond that, we don't know anything more," Briggs said. "What time did you say he was supposed to be at your place last night?"

"I was expecting him by about 8:30 pm. I spoke to him at eight and he said he needed to get some things together and he would be right over," she explained.

"Okay, that's good to know, I'll keep you posted if I hear anything else," Then he hung up.

If she needed any more proof that she was way over her head, she had just received it. Poor Nate, he had stuck his neck out to give her a hand and now he was dead. On the positive side, the FBI was now involved and she felt confident that his case would be investigated thoroughly. And she was also sure that the special agents would be looking for information back at Nate's office to see if his death was tied to the case or not. The bodies were beginning to stack up and she couldn't help but wonder if she was going to be the next one.

SHE COULDN'T EAT ANYTHING for dinner as she just didn't have an appetite. The waiting and not knowing what was happening was so hard. She knew the agents and Briggs were busy with Nate's death and that they would contact her as soon as they were ready to do anything, but that didn't make the waiting any easier. And she couldn't help but think that she had actually been doing a lot of waiting lately.

When ten o'clock came and went, she decided to go to bed to try and get some sleep. She was hopeful that tomorrow they would be able to move forward with their plan to bait the bad guys. Rebecca was able to fall asleep but it was a light, disturbed sleep that was punctuated by strange dreams. Jason visited her to let her know he was okay with her being gone as he didn't really need her at home. He walked away with a woman dressed as a maid who was holding a duster and cleaning a miniature version of what Rebecca somehow knew was Nate's car. In another dream, Sheriff Briggs was telling everyone that Nate had killed himself because he was Natalie's boyfriend.

Then, Frank, the window repairman ran around trying to swat at teenagers with a huge piece of glass. When she woke, her hair was damp from sweat and the sheets were tangled around her legs. So much for a good night's sleep, Rebecca thought to herself. She might as well have stayed up for all the rest she had gotten.

Looking into the mirror in the bathroom, she took in the dark circles under her eyes and the beginnings of a vertical line between her brows. Her sister's death had taken its toll and she figured she looked ten years older than when she came to Spenser. She splashed water on her face and brushed her teeth. She wasn't sure when the FBI agents would be ready to set up things in her house, but she wanted to be ready when they were. She didn't want any more delays in solving her sister's murder.

She was glad she had gotten ready to face her day when, moments after she entered the kitchen and was making coffee, she received a text from Briggs. He wanted to know if they could come by the house to go over their plans. After making sure she had enough creamer for the coffee, she went over and unlocked the front door. She sliced some banana bread she had purchased the last time she got groceries. That seemed like ages ago, and her kitchen supplies were running low. Hopefully, this would be all done and wrapped up before she needed more.

She heard the loud truck pull up and she set coffee mugs and the bread out on the kitchen table.

"Come on in," she greeted them at the door. "I hope you drink coffee 'cause it's all I have."

Not long after they had all sat down at the table, Special Agent Rudder received a text message saying that the techs who were going to wire her house up were on their way and about forty-five minutes out of Spenser.

"The first thing we need to do is come up with a script of what you will say on the video," Reinhold jumped in. "I saw you already posted one after your sister passed away so I assume there will be no technology issues getting another one up?"

She shook her head no.

"Okay, we want to make sure you appear happy and not as terrified as you look now," he continued. She smiled ruefully at him. They might be used to all this cloak and dagger stuff, but she wasn't. While this may be another day at the office for the Agents, for her it was a surreal and terrifying experience.

"We also want you to make sure you say that you have the evidence in a safe place, so they know there is something tangible. If they think it is just in your head, their objective will be to kill you and we don't want that," Rudder said.

"Speaking of killing, do you know anything more about Nate?" She asked suddenly, horrified that she had forgotten to ask.

"We don't know a lot more than we did yesterday. It appears the car went off the road and straight down into the ditch with no brakes being applied. We'll know more once Cranston does the autopsy" Sheriff Briggs informed her, then he turned to the Agents to let them know that Michael Cranston was Spenser's Medical Examiner. He seemed pleased to be able to fill them in on Cranston's role, as though he was happy that at least there was something he knew that they didn't. They simply nodded that they heard.

"Poor Nate," Rebecca said as she stared off into space. She was remembering the terror she felt when her car began acting outside of her control and when she saw that brick wall coming directly at her. She shivered as she thought of what Nate's last minutes must have been like.

"There will be agents located at every entrance and exit to your street, someone will be watching the front, and another will be at the back. At night we will have the latest technology so we can see as clearly as possible. We will be able to see and hear anything that is happening in the house. I know this is extremely intrusive, but we need to use everything at our disposal to make sure you are safe because that is of the utmost importance to us. If at any time we become concerned about your safety, we will pull you out." Reinhold said the last sentence with a forceful emphasis, and she felt comforted by his words. She wasn't in this alone.

"Do you want us to help you do the video?" Rudder asked.

"No, in fact, if you can leave me alone in the house to do it, that would be really helpful," Rebecca said a bit shyly. "To be honest, my sister loved doing her videos, but I feel extremely self-conscious if anyone watches me tape something."

"That's not a problem, we have some business we need to tend to anyway. But please don't post it without us having a chance to see it first, okay? We want to make sure it has all the components we need."

Chapter Thirty-Four

She had jotted down a few notes of what she wanted to say on the video and had put some makeup on when the techs who were putting up the cameras and bugs arrived. They suggested it would probably be easiest if she waited outside. That way she would be out of their way as it was a pretty small house, but also, if she didn't know where things like the cameras were installed, she would be able to act more naturally around them. She heated up her morning coffee and went into the backyard to sit at the picnic table. She looked around the backyard and realized it was very easy to imagine Natalie here with her. The house, the backyard, it was all so Natalie. It fit her like a glove. It brought Rebecca some form of solace to realize that although her sister died before her time, she had lived a life that was just what she wanted.

In a remarkably small amount of time, the tech guy poked his head out the back door and told her they were finished. When she entered, they had packed up their stuff and were heading out the front door. She assumed they were used to installing things like cameras and microphones very quickly. She couldn't help but be amused by this surreal world she suddenly found herself living in.

About an hour later, her video finished, Rebecca sent a text to one of the agents to let him know it was ready to be reviewed. Special Agent Reinhold was on the front step within five minutes, leading her to believe they were working not far away.

"I hope it hits the right tone," Rebecca said self-consciously as she hit the play button.

The video began with Rebecca thanking the viewers for leaving such lovely messages of condolence and that it helped to know that her sister had made such an impact on people and was loved by so many. Then she smiled brightly, as though she could barely contain her excitement. Because of their loyalty to her sister, she wanted them to be the first to know that she had made a major breakthrough, not only in her sister's death but in the last case her sister had been working on, the Sarah Jane Montgomery case. She had come across some evidence that was going to cause a huge stir, so get ready for a major disclosure, and possibly arrests in the next couple of days. She had come across some explosive evidence. And while it was in a safe place now, she planned on taking it to the authorities as soon as she was able to contact someone she could trust at the FBI. Because this wasn't something for the local police to handle, it was too big for that. She ended the video with another heartfelt thank you and a promise to keep them posted on any developments.

Reinhold had a big grin on his face as the video ended and he looked at her sideways. "That wouldn't have been a poke at the local Sheriff, how would it?"

She just smiled and said nothing.

"Well, it's perfect, how long will it take to post it?" he asked.

"Not long I don't think. My understanding is that the longer the video the longer it takes to upload, but this is pretty short," she explained.

"Okay, can you please let me know when it goes live so I can alert the team? I want everyone prepared to move as I suspect they won't take long to react," he said.

She prepared the video to post on her sister's YouTube channel but at the last minute, her finger hovered over the final keystroke. Was she doing the right thing by putting herself in this spot? But once again she came to the same place when she ran around in this thought circle; she couldn't not take the chance to find out what happened to her sister.

She touched the key and posted the video. She leaned back in her chair, closed her eyes, and breathed deeply. There was no stopping it now. She sent a text to both Agents to let them know it was going to go live in the next five minutes or so. She didn't send one to Sheriff Briggs.

A few minutes later her phone buzzed with an incoming text from Reinhold. "We checked and the video is live, everyone is set up and in place and the technology in the house is working."

Now, all she could do was wait.

THE REST OF THE DAY was uneventful, and it gave Rebecca some time to get used to the idea that other people could see her and hear her at all times. If she was honest, it was a bit exhausting, especially for someone with such strong introverted tendencies. It was like being 'on' all the time. She caught herself starting to sing to herself while she was making her dinner. She started to giggle and apologized out loud saying "no one needs to be subjected to that."

After she made herself something for dinner, she decided to see if there were any interesting comments on the video she had posted. Many of the subscribers were encouraging and quite pleased to hear that she had found something that was going to help the Sarah Jane Montgomery case. Although there were also quite a few questions about her sister, such as one asking her if that meant her sister had been murdered. She had been vague with both videos she had posted and hadn't made any reference to how Natalie had died, so she wasn't surprised there were questions. Most of the comments asked her to let her know more about what was happening as soon as she could. She was several scrolls into the comments when she saw a name that turned her blood cold. There was a comment from the person who had sent her sister the hate mail — exfan666.

"I'm so excited (not) to hear that things are going so well for you (gag). You sound just like your pathetic sister - look at me! I'm so great, look at me! Why don't you just rot in hell."

There were several people who responded to the comment, admonishing the person for their insensitivity and nastiness. They said they were going to report the comment, or they had already done so. Rebecca quickly got a screenshot of the comment in case it was pulled down. She sent the screenshot to Agent Reinhold via text. He responded immediately to let her know he appreciated her sending it, but it had already been flagged as they were watching the video carefully.

It was all she could do not to vocalize her frustration. What was she supposed to do? Sit around and twiddle her thumbs? She had gone from being the only one working on this to not being needed at all. Well, that wasn't entirely true: they needed her for bait, she thought rather ruefully.

She got up from the computer and flopped on the couch. Grabbing the remote she turned the TV on and flipped through several channels. She watched a show where someone was trying to convince their girlfriend that they didn't care at all about that other girl, she was the only one. Then the other girl came in the room throwing things and... Rebecca flipped the channel to the news; like she didn't have enough drama going on in her life, she didn't need to watch it on TV. Eventually, she landed on a home renovation show and she was able to turn her mind off for a while. She and Natalie had always been big fans of home renovation shows, although Natalie complained that each show that they watched gave her new, and sometimes contradictory ideas for her own house.

Finally, at eleven o'clock, she decided it was time to give it up and go to bed. It wasn't until after she had brushed her teeth and washed her face that she realized she wasn't sure if there were cameras in her bedroom or her bathroom. Was there a place she could change that was safe from prying eyes? She groaned quietly to herself. She sure hoped this was resolved quickly because she wasn't sure she could handle this much longer. Finally, she compromised by quickly removing her t-shirt and sticking her neck through her pajamas, and then removing her bra before slipping her arms into the armholes. She felt like she was back at camp again where she had felt as though she would be mortified if anyone saw too much. She slipped out of her jeans and into her pajama bottoms. There, problem solved, she thought with a small sense of control and autonomy in an otherwise uncontrollable situation. She turned the light off and crawled under the covers. She lay there and wondered if they could see her in the dark. Would they be able to watch her sleep? She really should have asked more questions.

Her restlessness the night before had apparently caught up with her and she was soon sound asleep.

Chapter Thirty-Five

H er legs swung over the side of the bed, and she sat up. Her heart was beating so loud and so hard she could have sworn it was now in her head. She was sure anyone within a few miles would be able to hear it. Why was she awake? She sat there, trying to calm her breathing and settle herself. She reminded herself that she wasn't alone, and she was being watched by highly trained agents. But it was the middle of the night, they could have gotten tired and fallen asleep. No, don't think that way she scolded herself. She couldn't hear anything, but she was aware that the very air around her seemed to be full of tension, charged with something she couldn't quite put her finger on.

When her heart had slowed, and she felt like she had control of her breathing again, she stood up and quietly walked to her bedroom door. She turned the knob slowly so as not to make any noise. The house was old and tended to creak when she least expected it, but she hoped if she just went slow enough, she would be okay. In the back of her mind, she imagined the agent assigned to watch the cameras in her house watching curiously as she suddenly got up and started wandering cautiously around her house. They must be having a good laugh at the jittery woman. She told herself this, but in truth, she knew the agents took their jobs much more seriously than that.

She had the bedroom door open now and she cautiously moved into the hallway. Should she check out the bedroom first? Or would that just be cornering herself? Shit, why hadn't she asked more questions when she had experienced agents sitting at the kitchen table? She didn't know what she was doing, she was in way over her head.

What if she screwed everything up and because of her they couldn't get to the bottom of who killed Natalie? The dialogue going on in her head was going to drive her crazy.

She decided to head down the hallway towards the kitchen, she wasn't sure why, but it felt like that would be the logical place for an intruder to be situated. She had only taken a couple of steps when the world went black.

Chapter Thirty-Six

She awoke with an excruciating pain in her left hip. Her head bounced and hit something next to her. What the hell was happening? Where was she? Her hands were behind her back and her feet were bound. There was nothing blocking her vision, but unfortunately, there was nothing to see but blackness. As she gathered her wits, she realized she could feel a humming below her that reminded her of car trips when she and Natalie were little. She was in a car. The air smelled dusty, and it was tinged with just a small amount of gasoline and maybe grease. She tried to keep track of how many times they turned but she had no idea how long she had been unconscious. How far had she been taken before she even woke up? Each pothole brought more pain as her hip continued to absorb her weight as she landed. Were the agents following her? Did they know what had happened? They had mentioned being able to track her phone if necessary but what if she didn't have her phone on her? Somehow, she doubted that whoever had kidnapped her had bothered to grab her phone for her before throwing her in a trunk and taking off.

She began to shiver slightly as the night air seeped through her pajamas and she kicked herself for at least not sleeping in something warmer. Just then, she felt the car begin to slow down, but the road they turned onto appeared rougher and she found herself being tossed to and fro even more. Damn it, if she made it out of this alive, she was going to be all black and blue. The car slowed down and stopped. As much as Rebecca had wanted the jostling to stop, she wasn't sure this was going to be any better. Now she could hear men talking and she couldn't help but wonder what they had in store for her.

A piercing shaft of light fell across her face as the trunk lid opened. Squinting, she looked up into the face of a dark-haired man who, if his all-black attire meant anything, was one of her kidnappers. Standing next to him was a short, squat man dressed in khakis and a stained white t-shirt, holding a gun that appeared to be the size of a large log. She had to tear her eyes away from it; she didn't want them to know how terrified she was right now. While Special Agents Rudder and Reinhold had seemed confident they wouldn't hurt her before they tried to get the evidence from her, she wasn't feeling so sure. What was to stop them from just shooting her outright, dumping her body, and being done with it? If this Alexander guy was as rash and unstable as they seemed to think he was, how could they be so sure what he would do? She kicked herself once again for not asking more questions of the Agents when she had the chance.

The dark-haired man grabbed her by her arm and dragged her out of the trunk. She immediately fell face-first onto the ground, unable to stand with both her legs and feet so tightly bound. She yelped and spat out the dirt that had made its way into her mouth. Once again, her arm was grabbed and she was flipped onto her back. The man who had hauled her out of the trunk approached her with a huge knife in one hand and she shrunk back. He reached down and sliced through the plastic ties on her legs, chuckling as though he enjoyed the look of fear on her face. He helped her to her feet, and she looked around with interest. She didn't know the area well, assuming they were still near Spenser somewhere, and this place seemed to be remote. The car they had arrived in was parked on a gravel driveway that came up to what appeared to be a cottage. For the first time, Rebecca realized she could hear waves splashing in the distance. She was at a cabin on a lake, from what she could tell. Should she try and say something about where they were in case the Agents could hear her? No, she had to assume these guys were not total morons and would pick up on her describing their whereabouts. But it was so quiet as a light breeze made the treetops around them dance. Where could the Agents be right now? Were they out there watching or had these men managed to lose them?

"Get a move on!" The man with the gun who was coming up behind her poked at her back. She didn't want to look and see if it was the gun he had nudged her with or his finger. It was best if she didn't think too hard about how close that gun was to her. They took her up two steps and through a side door of the cabin. When they entered the cabin, it was almost directly into the kitchen. The man in front of her kept walking but she wasn't quite sure what to do, should she follow him into the house even further? The man behind her had stopped walking and just stood there.

"What's your name?" Rebecca asked the man with the gun. As soon as she asked the question, she realized how stupid it must sound. As though he would give her his name. Why not his birthdate and social security number too? The man must have been thinking the same thing because he frowned and looked at her as though he wasn't sure what planet she was from.

"Call me Nightmare," he finally said, grinning wide enough that his crooked, darkened front tooth showed. It was then that Rebecca had a horrifying realization. Neither of the two men were covering their faces. They didn't care if she could identify them. She was new to all this cloak-and-dagger stuff, but even she knew that wasn't good.

Just then the first man returned and motioned for her to follow him. They went down a narrow hallway that opened to a large room that had a loft overlooking it. There were two large couches and a couple of casual chairs that looked as though they had come from someone's basement. They faced a large TV that was mounted on an opposite wall. The other wall had one of the longest desks Rebecca had ever seen and several monitors were mounted on the wall above it. The video on the monitors looked like a very high-tech security or monitoring system. There was a man sitting at the desk with his back towards them and Rebecca stood awkwardly in the center of the room, waiting to be acknowledged. After a couple of minutes that seemed like hours, the man turned around to face her. She gasped at what she saw.

"Why Rebecca, are you that excited to see me?" he asked. "Or am I not who you expected?"

Chapter Thirty-Seven

She tried to take the shocked look off her face, but she knew she wasn't doing a great job. If she had passed him in the street, she would have discreetly looked the other way and tried not to show any reaction. But in these circumstances, she was too scared to be polite. Because the man who stood in front of her had horrible burns on the left side of his face and half his nose appeared to be completely missing.

"Don't worry Rebecca, I understand," he reassured her. "You were expecting some smooth Italian mobster or even a swarthy drug cartel kingpin. Instead, you got the sideshow freak."

"No, I... it's just..." she stammered. "I was surprised, that's all."

"Yes, I'm used to surprising people," he stated. "Now, why don't you have a seat, and we can chat a bit?"

Now that her shock at his appearance had worn off, she looked at him with a more critical eye. His clothes fit him well and although she wasn't an expert in these things, she could tell they weren't cheap. He wore black pants and a form-fitting buttoned down white shirt. He tugged his French cuffs towards his fingers as he sat down, and she had the feeling it was a habit rather than an intentional move. She struggled to sit down without falling as her hands were still tied behind her back.

"Oh my, Darrell! Come and help our guest untie her wrists," he called out and snapped his fingers at the same time. A few seconds later she was sitting and rubbing her wrists as the blood began to pour back into her fingers.

"There you go, I hope you are comfortable now," he asked her with a smile.

"As comfortable as anyone can be who was kidnapped out of their bed in the middle of the night," she answered, immediately regretting her sassiness when she saw the roll of thunder pass over his face. She held her breath as he stared at her intently.

"I can see you have no regard for the niceties of civil society Mrs. Robertson," he said icily. "I guess we will just have to get straight to the point then. You have something that I need. I want you to give it to me."

She stared back at him. She realized she probably appeared defiant, but in fact, she simply didn't know what to say. They hadn't talked through exactly how she should handle things once they had drawn him out. Did they expect her to get some kind of confession out of him? If so, about which one of his illegal activities? These thoughts went through her mind in a flash before she decided. To hell with his other crimes, she was only interested in one. "Why did you kill my sister?"

"Now what makes you think I killed your sister? I'm told it was a double suicide. Very, very sad," he shook his head back and forth as though he was truly sad about it.

"My sister would no more kill herself than I would. I don't know how you did it, but I know you killed my sister because she was getting too close to uncovering some of your crimes," she plowed on. "I want to know if that is true and if so, how you managed to make it look like a suicide."

"What does it matter to you? Your sister is dead; how or why is irrelevant, isn't it?"

"No, it's not irrelevant. It's important to me to know the truth and it's important to Peter's mother to know if her son killed himself," she said.

"Oh, make no mistake, Peter killed himself," Mordaugh stated emphatically.

"He did?" She wasn't sure whether she should believe what he told her or not. "Did he also kill my sister?"

"Well, that depends on how you look at it."

"I don't understand," she said.

"I know you don't, but first you have something you want to give me."

She stared at him with a challenge written across her face. "Tell me about my sister and I'll give you what I have."

"Or... you give me what I want and then I'll tell you what happened to your sister?" he said in a sing-song voice, as though they were playing a game. She wasn't in the mood.

"Because if I do that, we both know you will kill me before telling me anything," she responded. "You will kill me tonight anyway, but I want to know what happened to my sister first."

He looked at her with what she could only describe as admiration; he was impressed that she knew she was going to die but she was not going to grovel, she was going to get what was so important to her before that happened. He thought for a moment before standing up and beckoned her to come with him to the long desk. He clicked on a few files and multiple videos began playing. There were several of her sister, but others of women who resembled her a bit.

There were videos of Peter and other men talking. Alex turned the volume down so he could explain what she was seeing.

"Technology is amazing these days, there isn't much you can't do with it," Alexander began. "Are you familiar with deep fakes?"

She shook her head no.

"It's where a photo or video is altered by artificial intelligence to create something that it isn't. Because your sister had so many videos posted and so many samples we could use, creating videos of her saying whatever we wanted and sending them to poor dumb Peter was easy." Alexander sounded proud of himself, as though he had created something wonderful.

"After lurking on her videos and her live streams, and checking out all the people who were commenting, we were able to pick out the most appropriate candidate to help us with the job we needed to be done. Peter was thrilled when deepfake Natalie contacted him. He had watched her for so long, and here she was, wanting to talk to him. She told him everything he wanted to hear," Alexander reached out and stroked a still picture of her sister that was displayed on his monitor. It was all she could do not to reach out and slap his disgusting hand away from her sister.

"It's really quite a shame you know, when she started looking into the Sarah Jane case. I wasn't too worried, we had covered our tracks very well, but then she started connecting the other ones. When Aleia reached out to her, we knew something had to be done."

"Aleia talked to my sister?" Rebecca was surprised she hadn't found anything that indicated they had met.

"Oh, she didn't talk to your sister, we made sure of that, but then she talked to you," he said the last as though he was resigned and that the situation was completely beyond his control. Rebecca frowned, uncertain as to what he meant. Why would he think she talked to Aleia, her sister hadn't even been able to locate her, even after asking her subscribers for help. Suddenly the puzzle piece fell into place, and she felt completely obtuse. Alexander watched as her emotions played out on her face and he began to chuckle under his breath.

"That's right, Emily is Aleia," Alexander confirmed. "She has been a thorn in my side for years, she has managed to elude us over and over again. My only consolation in not tracking her down is that she is spending her life on the run, never relaxing, or settling anywhere. She could have just done what she was told, made good money, and lived a contented life but she had to get all self-righteous, as though she wasn't the one who had taken that brat."

"I knew the only thing supporting it being a suicide was those stupid videos." Tears welled up in Rebecca's eyes. She had known all along her sister wouldn't have taken her own life but having it confirmed still felt like a weight had been lifted.

"Maybe she wouldn't, but he would, and he did," Alexander said. "He received a video from her telling him she wanted him to kill them both. There was only one weakness in an otherwise perfect plan, and that was what if she convinced him she didn't want to die when he showed up at her house?"

"What would you have done then?" she asked.

"Oh, Darrell's really good with Plan Bs," he said with a chuckle. "Darrell was watching to make sure it happened as it was supposed to and if it didn't, he would step in and finish it, then stage things afterward. But Peter came through for us."

Peter came through for them, Rebecca thought, lucky them. They had set the ball in motion and then watched it play out. Depressed, unstable Peter was drawn into a relationship with a make-believe woman he thought was Natalie, his YouTube crush. Then, when he was deeply committed to her, she asked him to help her, and he did. Her poor sister never stood a chance, and she probably had no idea what was happening when this strange man showed up on her doorstep acting like they were in a relationship.

"Isn't technology amazing?" He continued. "It used to be that a picture was worth a thousand words, then along came photo editing software and we couldn't trust pictures anymore. Now, with AI, we can't trust videos either. In fact, it makes you wonder if there's anything you can trust even when you see it with your own eyes, doesn't it?"

"I guess so," Rebecca said as she walked back to the couch and sat down. "But now, it's your turn to give me what you have," Alexander stated.

Rebecca looked at him, this man who was responsible for taking the most important person in the world from her. This was a man who had arranged for an innocent but ill man to take his own life, for Nate to be killed, and he had ripped babies from their families.

"I don't think so," she said, just as federal agents poured into the room, every gun pointed at Alexander.

Chapter Thirty-Eight

The U-Haul was almost full when Sheriff Briggs pulled up in front of Natalie Baker's home. Rebecca placed the last box on the pile and pulled the overhead door down and secured it.

"Got everything wrapped up?" he asked.

"Pretty much. I have someone coming to get the furniture and donate it to a women's shelter. I don't need it and I feel like it would make Natalie happy to know it went to people who would appreciate it."

"And your car?"

"Nothing much to say about the car except insurance will be paying me out, since it's not worth fixing," she explained. "I'll be in the market for a new one when I get home."

Sheriff Briggs stood looking at the house. He looked like he wanted to say something but didn't quite know how to get the words out. She decided she wasn't going to make it easy for him either.

"Well, I just wanted to let you know that everything checks out with the story he told you at the cabin, we found all the files on his computer and everything,"

"Okay, thanks."

"They also think they have some evidence to charge him with Nate's death as well," Briggs continued.

"What about the missing babies? What about Sarah Jane Montgomery?" Rebecca asked. "They'll be charged with those too, for sure, but as for finding the babies? That's going to be a bit harder. It's been years and so far, they haven't been able to find any records or information telling them where the babies went," he said quietly. "I only hope if they can't find them that it brings some peace to the families to know what happened and that their kids went to families who would love them."

She had a hard time believing he was naive enough to think that was the outcome for every baby taken by Alexander, but she wasn't going to be the one to poke holes in his fantasy.

"Listen, Rebecca, I'm really sorry I didn't believe you when you said your sister didn't take her life," he began. "But I really thought you were just in denial."

"Now, Sheriff Briggs, didn't your mother teach you that any apology followed by the word 'but' isn't an apology?" Rebecca smiled over at him, surprising herself with her willingness to let him off the hook. She was still unhappy with the way he had treated her, but she was too emotionally spent and tired to waste any more time holding a grudge.

"Yeah, yeah," he smiled back. "So, you headed back home now?"

"Yeah, I. have some business to deal with there," Rebecca wasn't about to explain things any further to Briggs so she bid him farewell and jumped in the cab of the U-Haul. With one last look at the home her sister had made and died in, she took off down the road. She was looking forward to the drive, some time to clear her head and decide what she was going to say to Jason. She didn't know if her marriage was over now or not, but one thing she did know was that whatever her future held, she was strong, resourceful, and resilient. There was no reason for her to remain stuck in a life that didn't fit her. In some ways, she felt that this realization was a parting gift from her big sister. Natalie had tried to tell her for years but now she finally got it.

"Thanks, sis."

Don't miss out!

Visit the website below and you can sign up to receive emails whenever CARLA HOWATT publishes a new book. There's no charge and no obligation.

https://books2read.com/r/B-A-BXIW-QZEEC

BOOKS 2 READ

Connecting independent readers to independent writers.

About the Author

Carla Howatt lives in Alberta, Canada where she helped raise three children, two husbands and a few pugs. A communicator at heart, Carla is also a proud introvert, port inhaler and dark chocolate hunter.

Her pets Carrera, Mercedes, Enzo and Mufasa keep her laughing and her husband keeps her shaking her head.

Read more at https://www.facebook.com/CarlaHowattAuthor.

CPSIA information can be obtained
at www.ICGtesting.com
Printed in the USA
BVHW070039160223
658635BV00001B/29